HOWL

SERENA VALENTINO

HOWL

EVERYTHING THE MODERN
WEREWOLF NEEDS TO KNOW

weldon**owen**

INTO THE WILD

Do you yearn for a life of freedom and mystery? Do aspects of human society strike you as flawed and phony? Then cast off the shadow of the human world and embrace an ancient and liberating magic. Discover the shadowy beast within you—become a werewolf.

Werewolves have fascinated and frightened humans for centuries. Whether sleek or savage, they embody primal instincts and supernatural talents that humans can only dream of. Strength, speed, and reflexes—not to mention pure animal magnetism—can become yours through lycanthropy.

Venture, if you dare, into an enticing new life filled with adventure, danger, and intrigue. Whether you choose to run wild with your brethren or roam the dark and misty roads alone, you are about to take the world by the throat.

This guide will help you seize everything the lycanthropic life has to offer. Engage your abilities; outwit your enemies; discover your history and your future. Embrace the wonders of the natural and the supernatural, the animal and the human, and the pure, raw power that only a werewolf can wield.

CONTENTS

Book Two: The Stylish Lycanthrope

Book Three: Moonlight Mastery

For Further Study

UNLEASHING YOUR
WILD SIDE

You stand at the crossroads, on the verge of prowling the moonlit paths of the werewolf—wild, free, and untethered by human restraints. If you dare to face your inner beast, an awe-inspiring transformation awaits.

In the pages that follow, you will learn the numerous ways one can become a werewolf, from traditional methods to obscure practices. You will discover the visceral feeling of this change (as well as what to expect from your new powers and instinctual gifts) and learn to recognize your shapeshifting brethren and evade the tactics of hunters.

As surely as the moon waxes and wanes, you will inevitably return to human form. This chapter will guide you on how to mix with humans and commune with other supernatural beings. And finally, you will learn the fine art of blending your human and lupine essences into a harmonious whole.

Your nature is one of duality—of beauty and horror, of savagery and nobility. Read on to embrace this fearsome destiny.

WEREWOLF ARCHETYPE?

Feeling a bit lycanthropic, but not sure exactly what kind of werewolf you've turned into? Or perhaps you're thinking of taking the plunge and wondering what you'll be like. Take this helpful personality quiz to determine your true werewolf persona.

1 HOW DID YOU BECOME A WEREWOLF?

A. You were born into an ancient and proud werewolf society.
B. You transformed unexpectedly after some vampires showed up.
C. You're still in denial about that strange animal attack. *A*
D. You're demon spawn.

2 WHAT DOES THE OPPOSITE SEX THINK OF YOU?

A. Your striking appearance and incredible strength both frighten and attract them.
B. To your frustration, they often just want to be friends. *B*
C. They want to help you.
D. If they have any sense, they flee at the sight of you!

3 WHAT DO YOUR NIGHTMARES TEND TO INVOLVE?

A. Being enslaved by vampires.
B. Seeing your friends get turned into vampires. *A*
C. Attacking innocent humans.
D. You are the reason humans have terrifying nightmares.

4 WHAT IS YOUR HUNTING OR FIGHTING STYLE?

A. You and your clan will fight to the death to defend yourselves.
B. You fight only to protect the ones that you love. *B*
C. You hate fighting but can't defy your nature for long.
D. Get as many humans as you can.

5 WHERE'S YOUR IDEAL PLACE TO LIVE?

A. With your clan in your spooky ancestral castle.
B. In a place of stunning natural beauty where you can roam free.
C. Splitting your time between your place in the city and your family's country estate. *C*
D. Anywhere you can attack as many people as possible.

6 WHAT DO YOU THINK OF HUMANS?

A. They matter little to you. Vampires, however, are scum! *A*
B. Humans are your friends, and you'll do all you can to protect them. A little kissing would be nice, too.
C. Tragically, you can't keep yourself from hurting them.
D. They taste like chicken!

7 WHEN YOU TRANSFORM, WHAT HAPPENS TO YOUR CLOTHES?

A. They merge into your sleek body when you become a wolf and turn back into slick club clothes on your return to human form.

B. You tie them to your leg before you transform so they don't get lost.

C. Much to your dismay, you often come to in the neighbor's garden wearing little except the remains of your underpants.

D. Who cares? If you need clothes, you simply steal them from a human who passes by.

IF YOUR ANSWERS ARE . . .

MOSTLY A'S:

You're a Lycan. You're a born warrior who has dedicated your life to fighting vampires and liberating your kind from their tyranny. Just as your world is dark and under siege, your relationships are passionate and dangerous affairs.

MOSTLY B'S:

You're a guardian wolf. Your instincts for loyalty and protection (plus your dashing good looks) make you very popular with humans.

MOSTLY C'S:

You're a wolfman, tortured by the pain you cause your loved ones and other innocent humans when the moon is full.

MOSTLY D'S:

You're the big bad wolf—a nightmare creature whose only goal is to infect as many humans as possible. Your disdain for humanity fuels your drive to rapidly increase the wolf population, mauling and slashing as you go.

KNOW YOUR
WEREWOLVES

There are countless werewolf breeds scattered around the world, and their history goes back to ancient times, when people first worshipped those humans who had the power and strength of beasts. For generations, werewolves have been prowling the countryside, slinking down old cobblestone paths, and terrorizing city streets. Wherever they go, tales of their appetites and ferocious powers spring up in their wake. Here are a few species who have clawed their way into legend.

WOLFMAN

He's all gentleman—until that time of the month. With two sides warring inside him, this werewolf is a very dangerous, though unwilling, killer.

Characteristics Walks upright, often wearing a good suit. His face and hands, however, are covered with fur, and his teeth are oh-so-sharp.

Origin Created by a bite from another wolfman, usually on a Welsh moor.

Fact This werewolf usually fights to overcome what he sees as a curse.

Transformation A wolfman always transforms during a full moon.

WOLFMAN

KITSUNE

This devoted she-fox guardian is a faithful friend to those she loves. But to the evil and greedy, she's a malicious trickster.

Characteristics The *kitsune* appears as a beautiful fox dressed in women's clothing or as a woman or girl with fox ears and a tail.

Origin Japan.

Fact This werecreature has a magical and superior intelligence that becomes more intense as she grows older.

Transformation A *kitsune* can transform into fox form as she desires, but not until she's one hundred years old.

KITSUNE

LYCAN

A race of immortal monster wolves, lycans are locked in eternal combat with their vampire foes.

Characteristics Muscular and fierce, lycans have short snouts and a terrifying appearance. As humans, they often favor attire crafted of black leather.

Origin Descended from William Corvinus, the first of their kind.

Fact They're the ultimate beasts, with remarkable strength, reflexes, resilience, speed, and regenerative abilities.

Transformation Lycans transform at will.

LYCAN

SKINWALKER

Some Navajo legends say these feared shapeshifters come into their powers after committing an evil deed, such as the murder of a family member.

Characteristics Skinwalkers can transform into any animal but commonly choose predators like wolves, coyotes, or bears. They are usually male.

Origin North America.

Fact Skinwalkers are able to mimic loved ones' voices in order to lure victims from their homes.

Transformation Witchcraft allows them to shapeshift at will.

SKINWALKER

VILKATAS

VILKATAS

Baltic fairy tales tell of these witchy women with the power to change shape into wolves.

Characteristics *Vilkatas* appear as natural wolves.

Origin The Baltic region of Europe.

Fact *Vilkatas* don't prey on humans and occasionally even bring back treasure.

Transformation *Vilkatas* must take off their human clothes before changing into wolf form.

NAHUAL

These sorcerers transform into animals to which they are connected spiritually. Their mischief includes stealing cheese from kitchen pantries and teasing women.

Characteristics *Nahual*s may appear as black wolflike creatures with glowing yellow eyes.

Origin Mexico.

Fact *Nahual*s live openly among humans, as fear of their powers keeps them safe.

Transformation *Nahual*s transform through magic.

NAHUAL

JÉ-ROUGE

Humans inhabited by these mysterious werewolf spirits transform involuntarily into bloodthirsty wolves.

Characteristics They usually appear as grainy wisps of black smoke, but they may also show up in the form of spectral black dogs with eyes that glow red.

Origin Haiti.

Fact *Jé-rouge*s will sometimes try to trick a mother into giving up her child.

Transformation *Jé-rouge*s transform their human hosts upon possessing them.

JÉ-ROUGE

17

EGYPTIAN WEREJACKAL

Not just anyone gets into this club. These jackal-like werewolves proudly trace their lineage back to the Egyptian god Anubis.

Characteristics Dead ringers for Anubis, they combine the muscular body of a man with the head of a jackal.

Origin Egypt.

Fact Werejackals are associated with the ancient *Book of the Dead*'s rituals for judging the human soul after death.

Transformation Their methods are a closely guarded cult secret.

EGYPTIAN WEREJACKAL

NEURI

The ancient historian Herodotus chronicled the Neuri's bad reputation. Hard-living, hedonistic pagans, Neuri are furthermore rumored to be cannibals.

Characteristics Dirty, ragged, and barbaric, Neuri in their wolf form sport black fur and red eyes.

Origin Northeast of Scythia, near modern-day Belarus.

Fact Shamanistic rites that use mystical magic allow them to shapeshift.

Transformation Neuri transform into wolves once a year.

NEURI

BROTHERHOOD OF LYCAON

These vile, murderous men have been transformed into wolves as punishment for their flesh-eating ways.

Characteristics Brown or black wolves, they are usually covered in blood and have a depraved temperament.

Origin Ancient Greece.

Fact The ancient Arcadian King Lycaon earned his wolf pelt when he served Zeus a dish of human flesh.

Transformation The transformation occurs after cannibalism and may last for seven years—or longer.

BROTHERHOOD OF LYCAON

KASHUBIAN SHAPESHIFTER

Some Eastern European children born with certain marks and signs, such as birthmarks or fur, have been able to shapeshift at will.

Characteristics Ethereal and childlike, the Kashubian shapeshifter is often mistaken for a changeling or faerie in human form.

Origin Northern Poland.

Fact These shapeshifters can transform into any animal but prefer the wolf form.

Transformation Can transform at will, although sometimes strong emotions, such as anger, trigger automatic transformation.

KASHUBIAN SHAPESHIFTER

DESCENDANT OF FENRIR

Terrible and cruel, these werewolves get a kick out of infecting humans. Their ferocity inspired Norse legends of warriors, known as berserkers, who fought as animals.

Characteristics They may appear badly scarred, and they have awful dispositions.

Origin Scandinavia, where Fenrir was born as a monstrous wolf to the shapeshifter Loki.

Fact Unlike other werewolves, Fenrir and his descendants crave blood even while in their human form.

Transformation Fenrir types use potions and animal pelts to shapeshift.

DESCENDANT OF FENRIR

GUARDIAN WOLF

Unless their people are menaced by vampires, the werewolf side of these loyal protectors lies dormant, sometimes for generations.

Characteristics Guardian wolves may be male or female. In wolf form, they are much larger than normal wolves.

Origin The Pacific Northwest coast of North America.

Fact Members of the pack can hear each other's thoughts and often communicate through telepathy.

Transformation They can instantly shapeshift at will, but sometimes their emotions trigger transformation.

GUARDIAN WOLF

TEENAGE WOLF

TEENAGE WOLF

These young werewolves find that their lycanthropy is an asset to them in high school, helping them excel at their favorite sports and win friends and admirers.

Characteristics In human form, they look like typical teenagers. In wolf form, they retain many human characteristics—walking upright, speaking, and even wearing their team uniforms.

Origin Found in many high schools.

Fact These werewolves enjoy all sports, but especially basketball.

Transformation Often involuntary, transformations involve sudden fur growth.

HOW TO GET YOUR
WOLF ON

Thanks to their long and varied history, werewolves have developed many ways to pass on their powers. While methods range from grisly to the fairly tame, they all lead to the same beastly result.

ATTACK

Simple and effective, this method is a particular favorite of traditional wolfmen. It involves a bite or wound that is deep enough to pass along the lycanthropic gift but not so serious that the victim dies. Needless to say, it's something of an imprecise science and a bit risky.

RITUAL

In many aboriginal cultures, rituals allow humans who share a spiritual connection with wolves to shapeshift. Typically, this involves removing your clothes and putting on a belt made of wolfskin. For best results, find an experienced shaman who is willing to help.

ENCHANTED WATER

Drinking rainwater from the paw print of a wolf is said to transform the drinker. Should you wish to try this nonviolent and rather beautiful method, bone up on your tracking skills.

MOONLIGHT NAP

In Germany, Italy, and France, humans who wish to turn into werewolves will sometimes sleep outside on a specific but little-known summer night during a full moon. The moonlight must shine directly on the person. While this custom is quite relaxing, it is not always effective. European werewolves in the know may be able to shed some light on this practice.

CANNIBALISM

Historically, people who dined on human flesh (or—even more gruesomely—devoured the entrails of small children) were turned into werewolves. Werewolves who live today usually don't resort to such extreme methods.

MAGIC

Witches and wizards can transform themselves or others into animal form. While some become wolves, they may also manifest as cats, coyotes, or other creatures.

RELIGIOUS OFFENSE

At one time, it was thought that people who died in a state of mortal sin came back to life as blood-drinking wolves.

FAMILY HERITAGE

If one or both of a child's parents happen to be werewolves, the child will inherit the gene for this condition. Signs of lycanthropy usually start to exhibit themselves around young adulthood.

PROTECTIVE INSTINCT

Some werewolves come into their true nature only when their loved ones need protection. If you find yourself adding muscle rapidly, running a high fever, and hearing the thoughts of the "pack" around you, your life is about to take a wild and furry turn.

SIGNS YOU'RE A
WEREWOLF

You'd think that something as momentous as becoming a werewolf would be hard to miss. But time and again, new werewolves are surprised at their own transformations. If there's a chance you're about to turn into a fearsome predator with insatiable appetites, wouldn't you appreciate getting a heads-up? Here are the telltale signs that your animal side is about to take over.

Spontaneous Muscle Growth

One welcome side effect of becoming a werewolf is a sudden toning and hardening of your physique. Have you developed muscles that you didn't know you had? Extreme and unexplained buffness can indicate a wolfish change to your physiology.

Fast-Growing Fingernails

You might notice that your nails are much longer than usual and that they grow back at a rapid rate, no matter how often you clip them. Does scratching the slightest itch bring blood to your skin? Maybe you need a moon chart more than you need another manicure.

Cravings for Very Rare Meat

Do steak tartare and beef sashimi have you salivating? If you've been lurking at your local butcher shop, either you're suffering from an iron deficiency or you may be turning into a werewolf in the very near future.

Fever or Night Sweats

An elevated body temperature can mean you're coming down with the flu . . . or with lycanthropy. When you become part wolf, your body responds by turning its metabolic fires on high. Night sweats—especially when paired with vivid hunting dreams—are another tip-off.

Vivid Nightmares

Lurid dreams about running through a forest are a classic sign of werewolfery. Do you have visions that you're taking down deer and devouring them in a beastly fashion? These dreams may leave you feeling disgusted yet strangely satisfied, especially if they involve hunting humans.

Violent Urges and Outbursts

Some werewolves report a growing sense of rage in the days and weeks leading up to their transformations. Savage moods can indicate you're on your way to some truly beastly behavior.

Excessive Hair Growth

Are you sprouting new hair? If you're male, do you suddenly sport aggressive facial hair growth, not all of it relegated to the upper lip? Certain medical conditions cause extreme hairiness in humans, but if this new hirsute you is an overnight change, suspect lycanthropy as the cause.

25

TRANSFORMATION:
THE GOOD, THE BAD, AND THE UGLY

Whether you're thinking about becoming a werewolf or you've recently joined the pack, you're probably wondering what it feels like when you change into wolf form (and what happens to your clothes). While some transformations are painful and devastating to witness, others can be enchanting and beautiful.

RIP AND ROAR

Werewolves who transform unwillingly or who are conflicted about their nature often have frightening and painful transformations. Your bones are stretched or compacted to fit a new wolfish frame. You howl in terrible pain, your skin rips, your teeth lengthen, and your whole face re-forms into a snout. Luckily for you, if this is your lot, you won't remember a thing when you wake up. Unluckily, you'll also be naked.

FUR SPROUT

Most common to adolescent werewolves, this type of transformation is guaranteed to happen at the most embarrassing moment possible. It's painless (except for the humiliation factor). Typically, you'll be in some public place like the school cafeteria—or worse, you'll be out on a date—when you notice the fur springing up on your exposed skin. Awkward!

LUPINE LEAP

Many packs that celebrate their werewolf identity have developed truly awe-inspiring transformations. If you're one of these types, you might shapeshift by running through the forest in human form, gathering speed, until an unearthly glow envelops you in mid-leap and peacefully transforms you into a wolf. When you land on your paws with utmost lupine grace, you continue to run wild and free under the moon. Your stylish duds will show up again when you come back to human form.

INSTANT WOLF

Some battle-hardened werewolves don't waste time with showy transformations. If you're a warrior or lycan type, you'll change shape with tremendous speed and little or no discomfort. In the blink of an eye, you'll become a monster wolf, ready for a fight. On the return trip, you'll have your clothes—and they'll be formfitting and attractive as always.

THE WITCHING WAY

Changing shape through witchcraft or sorcery involves shifting the mind or spirit first, then letting the body follow. As your psyche enters the animal realm, feelings of panic can rise up, making this type of transformation one of the most harrowing. When you return to human form, you'll often have a wolf pelt with you.

> Scene from *An American Werewolf in London* (1981)

ARE YOU A
MENACE TO SOCIETY?

For some werewolves, the morning routine involves looking down at bedsheets soaked in blood, stumbling to the mirror to see a face streaked with gore, and wondering what terrible thing has happened now. Most lycanthropes don't want to harm the ones they love (or innocent bystanders, for that matter). So it's your responsibility to determine how dangerous you are—and to take any necessary precautions.

1 DO YOU TRANSFORM TO PROTECT LOVED ONES?

If you transform specifically to help your brethren or loved ones, you're a menace only to the bad guys. Society can breathe easy—you're probably out there protecting it right now.

2 HAVE YOU EVER WOKEN UP COVERED IN BLOOD?

This is usually a sure sign you're up to no good as a wolf. However, you may not have hurt any humans. Zoo animals, family pets, or woodland creatures may be your unfortunate victims instead. To be absolutely safe, lock yourself up at the next full moon.

3 ARE YOU HAUNTED BY GHOSTS?

If the ghosts of your mutilated victims keep popping up unexpectedly and telling you to take your own life so you stop attacking people, you're definitely a menace. It's time to invest in a sturdy restraint system so you don't hurt any more innocent people. Seek counseling if the haunting continues.

4 DO YOU HAVE FREQUENT MEMORY LAPSES?

It's common for werewolves to wake up with no memory of their time as wolves. Memory lapses don't mean that you were out running amok, but they're not a good sign, either. Scour the news for anything that could be your responsibility.

5 DO REPORTS OF GRISLY DEATHS FOLLOW YOU?

Any news of unexplained and awful murders in your area should tip you off that you may be the cause of some serious carnage (unless, of course, there are other werewolves around). Lock yourself up for your next few transformations and see if the "serial attacker" goes away.

6 DO YOU THINK LIKE A HUMAN IN WOLF FORM?

Some werewolves are in control of their actions and retain their memories after transformation. If you're one of these gifted shapeshifters, take to the forests, mountains, or moors and enjoy!

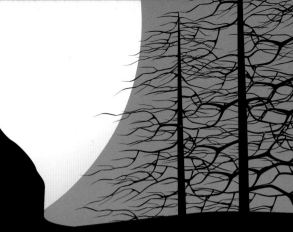

7 Do You Transform When You're Angry?

Too many werewolves have tragically hurt their loved ones while they were in the middle of a heated discussion or turned unexpectedly while under tremendous stress or pressure. Regular meditation practice—or some herbal medicines—may help. Sometimes just talking with a friend or a family member is all you need to keep a lid on your rage.

8 Do You Often Have Bloody Dreams?

If you frequently have dreams that involve killing animals in the woods or hunting humans on city streets, there's a strong possibility that these aren't dreams at all—in fact, they could be memories. Some further investigation is in order.

9 Are You Fighting Against Vampires?

A good vampire–werewolf feud can keep you busy and out of trouble for centuries, as long as there's not a love triangle involved. Most noble werewolf soldiers who are locked in this epic contest don't have time to pay humans much mind. Sometimes, however, you just need to create more werewolves for your army against vampires. If that's the case, don't worry about causing harm—your lupine recruits are on a path to glory. If a bunch of new werewolves is the price society has to pay to be vampire-free, then so be it.

10 Have You Woken Up Outside and Naked?

You're a menace to yourself. Start stashing some spare clothes in your territory and you'll spare yourself (and others) certain embarrassment. You may not be out there scaring and injuring people, but you do risk getting cited for indecent exposure if you go on this way.

SUPPRESS YOUR
WOLF NATURE

Lycanthropy can be a gift or a curse—sometimes it's all in how you look at it. For centuries, werewolves have been trying to suppress their monstrous urges, sometimes to no avail. Others have found creative ways to be a wee bit less . . . wolfish. Here are some tried-and-true solutions for the reluctant werewolf.

ENCHANTED ELIXIRS

Potions handcrafted by a trustworthy sorcerer can help suppress your transformations. Or look to a local apothecary for assistance in finding the right mix of herbal medicines for you.

SHACKLES AND CHAINS

Installing some sturdy chains and shackling yourself during the full moon is another sure way of keeping yourself and those in your environment out of harm's way. Just make sure to put your restraints somewhere out of sight—they might scare visitors who don't know your secret.

A PLACE TO HIDE

Building a "safe room" in which you can lock yourself has proven quite handy for some werewolves. Just make sure the lock is a hefty one. You don't want anyone to saunter in while you're in your wolf state—or when you've transformed back but haven't had a chance to put your pants on.

CHARMED!

Hide silver charms (a traditional means of keeping werewolves at bay) around locations where you often spend time. For certain werewolves, this can stop the transformation.

AVOID THE MOON

For some of you dear pups, simply staying out of the moonlight will prevent you from transforming. Keep an eye on the sky!

TEMPER, TEMPER

You may need to watch those emotional triggers. Try not to get so upset if your boyfriend is late for a date—you don't want to end up eating him by mistake!

EMBRACE YOUR
INNER ANIMAL

Tired of hiding in the basement and drinking smelly potions? Why not wear your fur with pride and enjoy the best of both worlds? In recent generations, many werewolves have embraced the beast within. Proud werewolves use these methods to make every night a full-moon party while still staying safe.

A Cabin in the Woods
Find a place deep in the woods where there are no other people around. Your rural retreat will offer the perfect place to frolic without fear of hurting humans.

Meditation and Yoga
The ability to clear your mind and calm your soul helps you control when and where you transform. Become a werewolf at your discretion. You'll impress your friends!

Hunt in Packs
Hunting in packs is one of the best ways to experience your new wild instincts! What is more thrilling than running free with your buddies?

Perfect Your Howl
This is one of the most satisfying ways to unleash your wolf nature. Just don't practice too much if you live in a city setting—you don't want to tip off hunters or vampires. A nice wooded area is the best environment for such things. When you get there, go wild.

Celebrate the Lunar Cycle
Make plans with your wolf pack to get together on significant dates like the full moon, the new moon, and the rare blue moon. Experiencing such events with friends is a surefire way to feel good about your werewolfery.

Parkour
You're bound to be great at parkour because your supernatural talents make you a natural. Plus, these skills may come in handy when you need to escape vampires or human hunters—and you'll look wicked cool.

HUNGRY
LIKE THE WOLF

You're a werewolf, and you're ravenous. But what should you eat? In the past, many werewolves snacked on humans. For most modern werewolves, though, the thought of eating people is a nauseating prospect. Here's how to avoid this plentiful but problematic food source while still getting the flavor and nutrition you crave.

EAT YOUR MEAT

The safest way to keep your legendary appetite in check is to fill up on high-quality protein before socializing with humans. For a carnivore like you, that means meat, meat, and more meat. Old-school werewolves may be into poaching, vermin-hunting, or other nasty dietary practices. Luckily, you have other choices.

BOND WITH A BUTCHER

As a newly minted werewolf, your best friend is the local butcher. Sure, you can always pick up a pack of frozen hamburger at the supermarket, but you'll be happier knowing that a trained professional is choosing fresh, high-quality cuts for you. Specialty butchers have access to a wider variety of meats, such as buffalo, venison, and mutton. For optimal health, try to approximate what an actual wolf might eat.

HUNT YOUR OWN DINNER

Wolves have superior hunting and tracking skills, so you will, too—even if your human form has a hard time sniffing out a good pizza joint. Keep your reflexes sharp and get some variety in your diet by hunting wild animals, as long as they're not endangered. In many highly populated areas, a lack of natural predators has created an overabundance of deer, turning them into nuisances. So by hunting them, you're actually helping to restore nature's balance! Avoid killing livestock, however tempted you may be. It's very unfair to farmers—and some of them may set out traps for predators or shoot on sight. Finally, watch out for those electric fences. You don't want to get your beautiful wolf coat all singed.

GO OUT ON THE TOWN

With a little planning, you can easily indulge your taste for raw or bloody meat when you dine out. Check menus for dishes like steak tartare (a dish of raw beef mixed with seasonings, onions, and often a raw egg). High-end restaurants will have delicious, better-quality meat, and eating it will make you appear sophisticated, not savage.

COOK AT HOME

When you invite human friends over for dinner, they'll be concerned if they see you eating raw meat (and telling them you're a werewolf won't help). Put them off the scent by searing your meat on both sides. If they ask why the inside is so bloody, say that you like your meat really rare. But do your human guests a favor and cook their portions thoroughly—they don't have the defenses against food poisoning that you do.

UNDERSTAND YOUR
POWERS

Werewolves have amazing supernatural powers, and each breed has its own set of strengths. Depending on your particular species, these are some of the talents you may expect to develop.

INCREASED STRENGTH

All lycanthropes benefit from enhanced physical force, some more than others. Few supernatural beings can rival a werewolf's sheer power in taking down its prey.

SPEED AND STAMINA

With intensified quickness, agility, reflexes, and endurance, you truly do have some superhero capabilities, remarkable even for supernatural beings. Many werewolves travel across great distances in a single night—in fact, in olden times, witches used to transform into wolves simply as a means of getting around. And with your superspeed, your movements will be a blur.

MIGHTY SENSES

All your senses are greatly enhanced. You can detect scents and sounds that are miles away and you have excellent night vision. Your superior tracking skills come in handy when you're pursuing those pesky werewolf hunters, vampires, and, of course, prey.

RAPID HEALING

Your ability to regenerate tissue while in wolf form means that it is nearly impossible to injure you gravely. This gives you an overwhelming advantage against enemies in combat—and makes wrestling with your pack more fun.

A TALENT FOR TELEPATHY

Some werewolves communicate with members of their pack by means of telepathy, and some can even hear the thoughts of humans. The constant background chatter is distracting at first, but many werewolves have been able to use it to their advantage.

TRANSFORMING AT WILL

Not all werewolves are lucky enough to possess this talent, and some work for the equivalent of many lifetimes to achieve it. Control over your transformations reduces the risk of exposure, and it sure helps if you need to summon up extra force when facing a deadly enemy.

FOREVER YOUNG

Most werewolves are slow-aging and long-lived. This makes them akin to vampires in the immortal domain (much to vamps' vexation).

MORE THAN HUMAN

Most werewolves possess supernatural abilities while in human form. Just be aware that some lose their self-healing powers when they change back. After running around as an untouchable powerhouse, coming back to your weak human state can be a letdown. It's a good idea to lay off the backflips until you know whether your healing abilities work between full moons.

SAVE YOUR PELT FROM
HUMAN HUNTERS

People get so uptight about a little animalistic behavior. Whether they fear or misunderstand you, humans aren't always happy to have a beast in their midst. Here's how to throw them off your trail.

KNOW YOUR ENEMY

In the past, everything from angry villagers to the Inquisition posed a threat for werewolves. Nowadays, your most serious enemy is often an obsessed hunter, working with the benefit of technology to track you down. The most dangerous kind has a personal vendetta against werewolves. Others are bounty hunters or vigilantes working for secret societies that hate supernatural beings. All hunters are dangerous.

HOW TO SPOT A HUNTER

Hunters are usually scarred and rugged in appearance, often with battle wounds on the face. They have a tendency to wear sturdy sport boots, gloves, and clothing made of leather, and they listen to classic rock bands. Some of these experienced trackers even achieve a kind of supernatural skill, developing a sixth sense that alerts them to a werewolf's presence.

HUNTING GEAR

Most werewolf hunters also have it in for other supernatural beings and travel with wooden stakes, holy water, or other means of killing vampires in the trunks of their cars. Alongside the garlic, expect to find a complete arsenal of antiwerewolf weapons, including silver bullets and animal tranquilizers. Savvy hunters may also travel with herbs and talismans known to render werewolves helpless. Some hunters who work

for rogue scientific organizations would love to get their hands on werewolf DNA. These types will have blood-testing kits on hand, as well as motion detectors, remote-controlled cameras, and night-vision goggles. If they can't capture you and bring you in, they'll be willing to settle for photos—for the time being.

THE TRAPS THEY SET

If you suspect you're being hunted, it's a good idea to change your routine and residence for a while. Hunters have been known to set up elaborate surveillance stations around a werewolf's home. Beware of any meat that appears unexpectedly around your den—it could be drugged. And at all costs, try not to get any wounds while in your wolf form. Hunters frequently try to "mark" a wolf and then see if a corresponding injury appears on the person they suspect of lycanthropy. Of course, if you're lucky enough to be a rapidly healing werewolf, this won't affect you.

USE YOUR TALENTS

For werewolves who have control over their transformations, the best advice is to stay human. Most hunters cannot sense you while you're in human form, and even those who can will have a hard time proving anything. For those who must change with the full moon, well, you've got those sharp teeth for a reason.

< Scene from *Son of Frankenstein* (1939)

TOOLS OF THE HUNTER'S TRADE

Werewolf hunters have a number of tricks up their dastardly sleeves. Since lycanthropes vary in terms of which substances can harm them, hunters avidly gather information and lore. This curious document was found among the personal effects of werewolf hunter Gareth LeStrange, who disappeared mysteriously one moonlit night in Wales. His body was never found, although some gnawed bones turned up years later near the site of his disappearance.

Basic Werewolf Tracker's Toolbox
Courtesy of the British Society for the Elimination of Lycanthropy

Silver in all its forms is effective against certain werewolf strains. Contrary to popular opinion, however, not all werewolves fear this precious metal.

Silver chains are helpful if you wish to capture a werewolf alive.

Silver amulets can ward off attacks, and crucifixes are not effective unless made of silver.

The classic silver bullet is great for long-range hunting.

Draw on the natural world for help combating shapeshifters. Several plants have proven highly useful in the field.

Mistletoe causes many European werewolves to back off.

Wolfsbane can calm wolves if the correct dosage is used, but too much may have the opposite effect.

Fresh rye plants cause some wolves to flee. In an emergency, hurl a loaf of bread at the beast!

SUPERNATURAL
FRIENDS AND FOES

There's no better friend than a werewolf. Once you've decided someone's worthy of your devotion, you're loyal to the end. But some members of the supernatural domain don't always play fair. Until you sniff out the truth about these creatures, you won't know if you've met an enemy or an ally.

VAMPIRES All bloodsuckers should be treated as enemies unless they have proven themselves worthy of your trust. Vampires' history of werewolf persecution speaks for itself. Still, some werewolves have been known to work with vampires against a common enemy. Some even have vamp roommates!

WITCHES Throughout werewolf history, witches have played a major role for both good and ill. In some werewolf packs, the elders pass down stories of beautiful women who lure men into the forest in order to transform them into wild beasts. But for every witch who's transformed humans against their will, there's another who's come to the lycanthrope's aid. Many modern witches live in harmony with werewolves, even helping them by concocting potions that make it easier for them to live in the human world.

GHOSTS You see dead people? Get used to it. Many werewolves experience a strong connection to the spirit world. Some ghosts can be friendly visitors who show up to guide you on your journey. Others are vengeful spirits who will taunt you and horrify you with images of your victims. Don't listen to the ones who tell you to end it all—they're just jealous.

DEMONS Mortals who oppose these universal foes can be turned into—you guessed it!—werewolves. If you were transformed into a werewolf at the hand of a demon, chances are you've got a burning hatred for all demonkind. Demons are known to intimidate werewolves and tempt them to be as murderous as possible. Steer clear of these bullies if you can.

FAERIES No matter how friendly faeries might seem, these exquisite magical beings are pranksters by nature. It's best not to let them get too close. Even a well-intentioned faerie can be bothersome—and some are terribly dangerous. The worst of these malicious sprites have powers that can easily send you running away with your tail tucked between your legs.

WELCOME
TO THE PACK

Wolves are social animals, and—for the most part—so are werewolves. Living with other werewolves can give you a sense of community, protection, and camaraderie. But, like any human family, a werewolf pack can also sometimes drive you nuts. Here's what to expect from your new furry family.

PERKS OF FAMILY LIFE

Maybe you were born into the pack, or maybe you were invited to join. Either way, you're now part of a group that has banded together for safety, survival, and companionship. So whether the clan lives in a gracious old mansion in New Orleans, a backwoods cabin in California, or a modern loft in New York City, your werewolf family always comes first.

LEADER OF THE PACK

At the top of the pack is the alpha, who is the commander or group leader (in a family pack, this will be a couple). In some packs, alphas are born into the position. In others, they ascend to the top spot by winning a challenge against the previous leader. Either way, the pack leader (and his or her mate, if one exists) is in charge of the entire clan and delegates responsibility to other members. If they don't show good leadership skills, someone else will come along and try to challenge them!

EVERYONE'S GOT A ROLE

Whether your pack is large or small, everyone in it has a job to do. Many packs include a wolf who is second-in-command, or beta. Children are sometimes looked after by an omega, a less-powerful pack member who nevertheless fulfills an important nurturing function. Except for very young members, everyone participates in group activities such as hunting.

ALPHA ETIQUETTE

If you have issues with authority, pack life will be a rocky road. In many packs, alphas get first dibs on food—and mates. They decide when and where to hunt, and whether to fight. In most packs, you'll need the leader's go-ahead on any big decision. This can be great if you welcome the guidance of your elders. But rebels who don't show proper respect will really ruffle some fur. Serious offenses against the pack or its leader are punishable by exile—or worse.

GOING IT ALONE

Maybe pack life isn't for you after all. If so, there's nothing wrong with striking out on your own. You might decide after a while to start your own pack. Or maybe you'll be happier if you give up on hanging out with werewolves altogether and concentrate on your human relationships. Many wolfmen find they're quite content as lone wolves. They prefer not to be with other werewolves because they're not that happy about their wolf side to begin with!

When you become a werewolf, your actions may well enrage many mortals, but many will also secretly desire your awesome powers.

> Scene from *The Wolf Man* (1941)

LUNAR CHART

FIRST QUARTER

Clear your social calendar. Tell friends that you've got stuff planned for the next two weeks or so in the evening, and ask them not to come over.

WAXING GIBBOUS

You should be starting to feel really wolfy around now. Your temper may get short, and you'l start craving red meat.

WAXING CRESCENT

Start preparing to transform. So many lycanthropes leave it to the last minute, and this can cause those annoying little slipups, like sprouting fur in math class. Do you have wolfsbane tea on hand? Stock up!

NEW MOON OR DARK MOON

Now is the time to do all the nighttime outdoorsy activities you want—your risk of transforming is virtually zero. Go for a romantic starlit walk, or take that camping trip.

Waning Gibbous

This will be a recovery period for you. For a couple of days, take it easy—watch movies, play games, whatever helps you chill. Clean up anything you broke or ripped up in your home.

Third Quarter

It's safe to go out at night again! See friends, go to shows, do everything your wolfy little heart desires. You deserve it after spending a couple of uncomfortable days in a bunker (or your mom's basement).

Full Moon

Lock yourself in a safe room. Make sure to leave a note for your friends or anyone who might come by that tells them not to enter. Say you have a terrible flu or are working on an important project.

Waning Crescent

See if you can get some friends together for a crescent-moon party on the beach or in the woods. There are so many full-moon parties that you don't get to attend (unless it's with your pack).

HIDING THE SIGNS FROM
HUMANS

Just because you're half human doesn't mean you've got a lock on mixing in human society. Here are some ways to hide your wolfy nature from people who aren't in on your secret.

SOCIALIZE WITH SAVVY

Gathering with friends and family should be fun. Just check your lunar chart before accepting invitations. (Goodness knows you don't want to transform right in the middle of Grandma's tea party!) And if you have a tendency to burst into wolf mode when you're upset, avoid stressful occasions or practice deep breathing to keep your cool. Nothing dampens a party quicker than a little mauling.

ACT HUMAN, PLEASE

Avoid animal mannerisms when you're trying to blend in. It's important not to growl or bare your teeth when expressing displeasure. And don't take it as a personal challenge if someone makes eye contact with you. Remember that humans don't normally go about on all fours, even if it does feel natural to you. And as for marking your territory . . . just don't.

SOUNDPROOF YOUR DEN

When you're in the privacy of your own home, it's perfectly all right to cut loose with a little howling now and then. But if you've got nosy neighbors, think about making an investment in soundproofing. Not only will they have no idea what's going on at your place every full moon, but you'll also be able to relax and be yourself without worrying about being overheard.

WEAR DOG TAGS

Find yourself a human you can trust, and make that person your emergency contact in case of unforeseen happenings. Be sure to wear some dog tags bearing your name, as well as the name and phone number of your contact person, in case you land in jail–or in the pound.

HIDE YOUR SENSES

Try not to react to every little smell and sound. Humans don't share your enhanced senses, after all. Your friends will think it odd if you go around sniffing bushes or fire hydrants. And you certainly don't want to acquire a reputation for "hearing things."

CONTROL HAIR AND NAILS

Some kinds of werewolves experience excessive hair and nail growth. Carry a razor and some nail clippers for quick grooming touch-ups when you're on the go.

KEEP CLOTHING STASHES

Hiding some clothing in a safe outdoor location is a good idea. You don't want to have to make your way home in a state of undress. Humans may not know enough about the supernatural world to suspect that you're really a werewolf when they see you outside without clothing, but they'll think there's something else wrong with you!

DATING
HINTS

Whether you're seeing a lycanthropic sweetie, a handsome human, or even an undead vampire darling, these tips will help you navigate the sometimes perilous world of supernatural dating.

DATING INSIDE THE PACK

There are definite benefits to dating one of your own kind. You're both on the same schedule, for one thing. For another, you'll always agree on what to eat. Just be sure to follow your pack's rules of conduct, such as getting the alpha wolf's or clan leader's permission before you start going steady. Lone wolves who want to cuddle up to a pack member should prepare to fight or challenge their way to a date.

SEEING ANOTHER SPECIES

Cross-species romance is always risky—but then again, werewolves aren't exactly known for playing it safe. Make sure you've found someone you can trust with your secret. You'll need to be open-minded about different cultural traditions, but with communication and lots of love, there's no reason you can't make it work with a human, a vampire, or even a witch. There is one case where it almost never works out, however: dating a vegetarian!

MAKE IT MEMORABLE

As a werewolf, you've got many ways to dazzle your date. Keep your love warm in the freezing cold with your luxuriant fur. Show your sweetie the beauty of the wonderful wild. If you're both werewolves, share a full-moon hunt or wrestle in the freezing surf on a deserted beach. If your love has any goth tendencies, he or she will appreciate a candlelight tour of your ancestral estate. Otherwise, camping trips, moonlight hikes, and wildlife-watching opportunities all make for a night to remember.

MEET THE PARENTS

As your relationship progresses, your beloved will probably want you to meet his or her family. Vampire parents may ask questions about your lineage and breeding, so come prepared to present yourself in a good light. Humans may be nervous about your potential for violence. Try to reassure them that your intentions are peaceful, and if possible, avoid encounters with the family pet. It won't help your cause when the cat hisses at you. Finally, you may be used to roaming all night long, but your human date probably has a curfew that you need to respect.

MATE FOR LIFE?

In the wild, wolf pairs are usually monogamous. Depending on your ancestry, you might end up seeking a lifelong commitment while some humans are still playing the field. Werewolves with strong instincts for loyalty and protection may find that they "imprint" on a particular person. This experience is like love at first sight (only stronger), and it lasts throughout the werewolf's life. Unfortunately, you can't predict or handpick whom you'll eventually imprint on. But if you're one of this rare breed, that special someone will really rock your world . . . forever.

THE STYLISH
LYCANTHROPE

You're a werewolf—you love your new life as a ferocious beast, and by all means you should enjoy it. So go ahead! Even werewolves need to let their scruffy hair down sometimes. Rebel against the brooding, agonized werewolf stereotype. Embrace the more lighthearted and frivolous part of your wolfy nature and have yourself some well-deserved fun!

Consider yourself charged with a most important mission: to show everyone in the supernatural world that werewolves really do know how to party. To assist you, this chapter features some dandy and exciting fashion tips that will ensure you look your best at those full-moon parties.

This chapter will also clue you into some deliciously dangerous decor ideas and a bit of costume and makeup advice for your human friends who would like to fit into your wolf pack. These are just a few tidbits of all that awaits your greedy consumption in the pages that lie ahead.

> Scene from *The Company of Wolves* (1984)

DEALING WITH
CLOTHES

You've just spent a liberating night romping about in wolf form, and now it's time to go back to being human. But when your human self returns, will it be wearing anything at all? Here's what you need to know about werewolves and clothing, along with some tips on how to make the return journey with your dignity intact.

MAGICAL CLOTHING

Some werewolves magically transform back into human form fully clothed. While it's not clear what accounts for this lucky convenience, lineage may be a factor. Lycans in particular are noted for this trait.

STRAPPING YOUNG LADS

Resourceful types may tie a little satchel that contains a change of clothing to their legs. That way, when they transform back to their human form, they won't have to find their way home naked—or pull an Incredible Hulk and steal from an unsuspecting neighbor's clothesline.

HIDDEN TREASURE

If you prefer not to be tied down when you go on a rampage, consider burying your clothes in a spot where you (and only you) can find them later. If you're the forgetful type, make yourself a little treasure map—X marks the clothing! A map is especially important if you can't return to human form without putting clothes back on (some werewolves are just that way).

TATTERED AND HUNKY

Upon returning to human form, you may find your clothing tattered but still functional. Keep in mind that rips and shreds aren't always a bad thing. Some people look great with their shirtsleeves ripped off and their trousers torn off below the knees.

OH, THOSE HIGHLANDERS

Scottish werewolves are rumored to sport kilts that they find themselves still wearing when they transform back. For safety's sake, if you see a wolf in what looks like a skirt, don't make fun of it. You might be getting in over your head.

STOCK YOUR SAFE ROOM

If you use a safe room, be sure to stock it with extra clothing. While this point may seem incredibly obvious, far too many werewolves neglect this very simple safeguard and appear in an embarrassing state of undress before their roommates, friends, or family members. Avoid this hairy situation with a little forethought.

STRETCH FOR SUCCESS

Some werewolves wear stretchy clothing so they don't rip their outfits when they transform. These types retain their clothing while they're in wolf form, rather like wolfmen. Consider having a custom outfit made so you can feel like a werewolf superhero!

WOLFMAN
MAKEUP TIPS

Chances are you've shared your secret with some human friends. Maybe they're curious about what it's like to go around as a werewolf, or maybe they're just dying to go to one of your amazing parties. Even though they can't transform into wolves, you can help them blend into the pack with these easy makeup tips.

WHAT YOU WILL NEED:

- Black and dark-brown matte eye shadow
- Fake hair that matches your hair color
- Hair spray
- Spirit gum

- Liquid latex and fake snout (for advanced use only)
- Long fake fingernails
- Black or dark-brown nail polish
- Fake fangs

EERIE EYES
Use dark-brown eye shadow to create dark circles around your eyes. Brush the eye shadow down to the tops of your cheekbones.

PREPARE FOR HAIR!
Nothing says "wolfman" like a thick coat of fur. You'll need some fake hair for your face and hands, as well as hair spray to volumize your own locks. You can find fake hair in most special-effects makeup stores, or you can buy a cheap wig. Cut the wig hair to the length you want, and put it aside for later application.

ROCK THAT FUR

Brush a light layer of spirit gum onto your chin, cheeks, and forehead, and then gingerly apply your fake hair on top, one layer at a time. Start from the bottom of your face and work up. You can adjust the length of the hair by trimming it after the spirit gum dries. Don't forget to make the tops of your hands hairy as well.

EASY WOLF SNOUT

You can make a wolf snout by marking the tip of your nose (including the rim of your nostrils) with black eye shadow. However, if you have access to a special-effects makeup store and you feel adventurous, you can create something more realistic looking. You'll need liquid latex and a fake snout. Follow the directions on the liquid-latex packaging for application.

SHOW YOUR CLAWS

Give yourself fierce claws by adding fake nails. Follow the directions on the nail kit to secure them to your own fingernails (most fake nails come with glue or have adhesive backs). After you've glued them in place, paint them with dark-brown or black nail polish. If you don't want to mess with fake nails, paint your own. For the final touch, pop in your fangs. You're set!

A leather or latex sleeveless T-shirt adds that goth-yet-tough-guy look.

Pull your hair into a ponytail to keep foes from grabbing it.

Leather motorcycle pants are practical and hefty wear for a warrior like you.

Sturdy leather boots with steel shanks offer support for all that running around.

FEARSOME FASHION:
LYCAN AND LEATHER

There is nothing more alluring than a dauntless, leather–clad urban werewolf. Try this arresting style if you feel that you belong at the heart of a stylish industrial pack. Whether you find yourself in a bit of a scuffle with vampires, prowling abandoned factories alone, or dancing all night at a warehouse party, you know you'll look good.

SLEEK BEAST

To achieve this smooth look, outfit yourself in dark clothing and metal hardware. Leather pants or black jeans are not only practical and sturdy for a warrior like you—they also look really hot. Top them off with a fitted black T-shirt (or a vampire-proof vest) to show off your animal physique. Subtle details like studs, buckles, and straps give your wardrobe a martial touch. Use a supple, formfitting leather jacket or long coat to complete your brooding ensemble. Flowing, wild hair reflects your inner wolf (but be sure to tie it back before getting into a fight—vampires don't fight fair and might use it against you).

ACCESSORIES

You'll want to wear motorcycle-style boots with tons of buckles and studs. To perfect your look, add some armbands or wrist cuffs (they'll draw eyes to your muscular arms). Try wearing an ancient medallion around your neck—it will cement your aura of long-prophesied bad boy.

LIFESTYLE

As a warrior wolf, you might spend your days training in martial arts and sparring. After long hours with your war council, you'll probably want to take your mind off military strategy and head to an underground rave or a secret live show. You're an urban animal, and in your leisure time you can be found skulking around cafés and cool clothing stores as well as the odd museum or two. (You never know what artifacts from your illustrious history you might happen to discover hidden away in a permanent collection somewhere.)

MUSIC

No easy listening for you: The music that soothes your soul sounds like noise to others. You favor the brooding, industrial attacks of Nine Inch Nails and Skinny Puppy, as well as the grandeur of classical tracks like Carl Orff's stark and harrowing "O Fortuna." In quieter, more contemplative times (perhaps as you consider how to crush your enemies), you might turn to Gregorian chants or Enigma's "Sadeness."

INSPIRATION

Werewolf warriors come from a complex and dark world, full of Gothic cityscapes and ancient strongholds. The Underworld film series is your cinematic touchstone, but you'll find hints of urban warrior style in movies ranging from *The Dark Knight* to *The Crow*.

STUNNING FASHION:
CUTE AND FOXY

Reveal your inner werefox with the adorable and sassy *kitsune* look. This style is eye-catching even compared to the most elaborately dressed supernatural beings. You can take this manner of dress in a traditional direction with a Japanese kimono or a contemporary school uniform, or make any dress foxy by adding a few accessories.

FOX-GIRL CHARM

A flowing kimono is traditional among *kitsune* and looks lovely when tied with a sash and bow in a striking contrast color around the waist. Faux cherry or apple blossoms in your hair recall the *kitsune*'s connection to bountiful harvests and will look beautifully delicate. For a more modern anime-inspired look, try dressing in a sailor-style school uniform with knee socks. Or go campy with a Sailor Moon cosplay dress.

ACCESSORIES

A fox-ears headband and a fluffy tail reflect your *kitsune* heritage even when you're in human form. And they're so cute! Ballet-style slip-on shoes will accentuate your graceful movements at school or on the dance floor.

MAKEUP

Your makeup can reflect your playful spirit as a magical *kitsune*. Try a light dusting of glitter for a hint of supernatural sparkle. If you're feeling more daring, go for a geisha look to play up your association with Japanese traditions. Use a white base makeup and powder, apply rosy pink for your cheeks, and finish with some very vivid red lipstick. Give yourself a black nose and whiskers with a bit of black face paint.

LIFESTYLE

You're equally at home in exquisite tea gardens and video arcades. More likely than not, you're reading manga and graphic novels and have strong opinions about your favorite anime. Plus, given your foxy reflexes, you're a whiz at games like *Dance Dance Revolution*. You're often found giggling with friends while shopping for an outfit, or quietly having a cup of green tea.

MUSIC

Your ease with experimental fashion is a gift you share with icons like Gwen Stefani and Lady Gaga. Chances are you're a J-pop fan and have singers like Ayumi Hamasaki and Utada in your collection, as well as groups like B'z. When you're in the mood for something even more evocative, try Ryuichi Sakamoto, whose music adds atmosphere to many films.

INSPIRATION

Kitsune characters appear in many books and manga, ranging from Masashi Kishimoto's *Naruto* to Neil Gaiman's Sandman series. While waiting to become a fully fledged fox-girl, draw inspiration from Harajuku street fashion and paw through Japanese folklore in books such as Y. T. Ozaki's *Japanese Fairy Tales*.

Geisha makeup and hairdos suit a tradition-minded kitsune.

In between transformations, wear a fox-ears headband.

Up your supernatural quotient with liberal applications of glitter in bright colors.

Loose knee socks are all the rage in Tokyo and conceal foxy legs.

Polarized sunglasses hide those telltale yellow eyes.

You never know when you might have to rescue a hiker. Or tie your clothes to your leg to transform!

A fitness watch lets you monitor your heart rate as transformation time draws near.

Sturdy hiking boots get you far off the beaten track.

FRIENDLY FASHION:
HUNKY NATURE LOVER

These handsome and sensitive wolf-boys make the ladies swoon with their innocent eyes, strong muscles, and reverence for nature. While many are hereditary tribal werewolves, bound to their land, others may simply feel a strong pull to the great outdoors. Embrace your woodsy side with this sporty, practical look.

NATURAL GOOD LOOKS

A good pair of jeans or hiking shorts will ensure that you're always ready to hit the trail. With your high body temperature, you don't need a flannel shirt to keep warm—but it does give a companion something to cozy up to. Keep your hair short and well groomed to set yourself apart from the other, gruffer shapeshifters out there. The clean-shaven look will reveal how much command you wield over your inner wolf.

ACCESSORIES

Polarized sunglasses not only protect your eyes—they can also hide your feelings if you find yourself getting too close to a human friend. A fitness watch lets you monitor your heart rate as you push yourself to your limits, and one with a good alarm system can help you keep track of when your transformation is likely to begin. It's a good idea to get yourself a light-weight pack filled with outdoor survival gear (it will come in handy if you meet anyone who needs rescuing). Lastly, rugged hiking boots help you travel far from human settlements.

LIFESTYLE

You're an easygoing dude, up for just about anything—though your preferences are for extreme sports and eco-tourist vacations. You might go mountain biking and cook dinner with friends or head to a coffeehouse for an acoustic open-mic night. You love to venture off the beaten path and are drawn to activities like rock climbing, sea kayaking, and snowboarding. But you're also a great cuddler and an expert maker of hot cocoa. Of all the werewolf types, you're the most likely to own a big, friendly dog.

MUSIC

Big, outdoor music festivals are a favorite of yours, as are groups that play extended live jam sessions, like Phish. Instead of hard-edged metal or industrial bands, you tend to favor indie-rock singer-songwriters or alternative folk acts. Try some Built to Spill or M. Ward to round out your music collection. Or simply get out your own acoustic guitar and write your own songs. There's more than one way to howl at the moon.

INSPIRATION

Your senses are very attuned to the natural world. Even when you're not outdoors, you can find a thrill in classic adventure stories like *White Fang* and *My Side of the Mountain*. Feed your need for adrenaline with literal cliffhangers like the movies *Vertical Limit* and *Touching the Void*. And when you're in a mood for guilty pleasures, watch some old seasons of *Land of the Lost*.

FEARLESS FASHION:
WARRIOR PRINCESS

Lady werewolves are just as fearsome as their male counterparts, so why not reflect that in your look? If you're ready for some action and attention, let out the barbarian she-wolf inside you. You'll turn heads and inspire puppyish devotion with this style, whether you and your savage entourage are out for a night of pillaging . . . or club-hopping.

WARRIOR WEAR

A gladiator-style overskirt works well for this look—it takes you from the dance floor to the battlefield without slowing you down (or sacrificing style). Wear it over leggings for extra modesty. A thick vest or leather corset offers protection from your enemies. And why not try donning a faux-fur vest? It will provide warmth without hindering you as you reach for weapons.

ACCESSORIES

Gauntlets help guard your wrists when you engage in swordplay, and a headband or scarf keeps your flowing locks under control while battling vampires. It's tempting to add heels with such a sassy look, but remember—you're going to be delivering karate kicks to the head. Balance is key!

MAKEUP

Your makeup can be as dramatic as you like with this look. After all, no one tells a barbarian wolf-princess that she's overdoing it. Try bold streaks of war paint on your face if you think there's a chance you'll be heading into battle. Otherwise, you might use bronzer (if you're pale) to give your skin a burnished glow. Black liquid eyeliner on your top eyelid and eye pencil on your lower lid enhance your imperious stare.

LIFESTYLE

When you're not training or fighting, you're hanging with your comrades-in-arms. Your pack is close-knit and loyal, and you might spend your time feasting with them, exploring the world of role-playing games, writing songs about your exploits, or going to the concerts of visiting troubadours. Being a warrior woman doesn't mean you can't have a boyfriend—just find one who appreciates your strength!

MUSIC

Your taste tends toward slinky Middle Eastern melodies, dance music from northern Africa, and battle-worthy industrial noise. Try some dreamy Arabic pop tunes from Amal Hijazi or the Algerian *raï* of Khaled. When you need to send your followers into a frenzy, reach for something like "Khyber Pass" from Ministry.

INSPIRATION

There are lots of places to find pointers on every aspect of style and strategy. Try watching the TV series *Xena: Warrior Princess.* Learn the finer points of warrior mythology by studying Amazons, Viking shield maidens, and Valkyries. Finally, search out books with female fighters for stirring bedtime reading. You'll find cool ladies even in classics like the Lord of the Rings series.

A headband or scarf can keep your hair out of your eyes should you get into a fracas.

An armored bodice or corset offers protection from your enemies.

Gladiator sandals or tight-fitting leather boots will ensure you look good while you kick butt!

An overskirt slit to the top of the thighs lets you move with great agility.

IDENTIFY YOUR
INNER WOLF

How do you know what sort of wolf you'll be when you transform? Interestingly enough, your personality often influences how you appear in wolf form. Use this reference guide to learn about some of the more common wolf types, along with their associated characteristics. Now you know what that cute gray wolf might be like as a human!

STRIKING WHITE WOLVES

Arctic wolves are snowy white with sleek, strong frames and glowing, light-amber eyes. Don't let their looks fool you—in the wild, Arctic wolves live and thrive in some of the toughest conditions on earth, and they're regally strong and stealthy. White werewolves are proud and unafraid, used to ruling their northern territories without human meddling. As humans, they may appear aloof at first. That beautiful blond werewolf girl sitting in the corner reading her graphic novel (and really taking everything in) more than likely transforms into one of these striking beauties.

BIG, BRISTLING BLACK WOLVES

Large, imposing, and dangerous-looking, black wolves stand out wherever they go. In the wild, true black wolves are rare, but the genetic adaptation that turned their fur black lets them hunt and hide sneakily in dark forests. If you encounter a werewolf version of a black wolf, know that you're dealing with someone even further out of the ordinary than the usual werewolf. It's often large and mysterious men with dark skin, wild hair, and beards that appear in the guise of a black wolf when they transform. Treat these types with respect.

MAJESTIC GRAY WOLVES

Regal and inspiring, gray wolves with piercing golden eyes are the most common wolf type and are found around the globe. The most mentally well-adjusted werewolves often manifest as gray wolves. Consummate hunters, protectors, and providers, these werewolves prefer spending time with their loved ones over fighting. If you see a group of young, attractive, strong, and free-spirited lads and ladies hanging out, it's likely that, if they're werewolves, they transform into majestic gray wolves.

RAGGEDY COYOTES

Skinny, weather-worn, and supersly, clever coyotes are adept at scavenging and always seem to land on their feet. Although they don't join groups as easily as gray werewolves do, werecoyotes will befriend other werewolves and humans in their travels. The coyote has quite the reputation as a trickster in American Indian legends, signaling its questioning nature. Humans who manifest as this animal usually like indie music, film, and fashion. That slightly tatty, handsome young gentleman at the back of the café reading Oscar Wilde or listening to Nick Cave on his headphones just may be a werecoyote in human guise.

CHOOSE YOUR
WEREWOLF NAME

What's in a name? When you're a werewolf, your name can convey your lineage, your hunting prowess, or simply your connection to an ancient mythological tradition. Some werewolves decide to rename themselves as a way of embracing their newfound supernatural life. Read on to discover a werewolf name that speaks to you.

CHOOSING YOUR NAME

Some werewolves select names for themselves based on their interests or research, or just because they like the way one sounds. If you're in an informal pack or clan, or if you're a lone wolf, feel free to choose a new name anytime. Start using it immediately, or hold a naming ceremony for yourself.

NAME SOURCES

World mythologies are a good place to start when you're looking for your werewolf name. Your human ancestry may lead you to embrace a name from a particular cultural tradition. Or search ancient languages for a word that has significance for you. For further inspiration, consider the name of a favorite legendary hunter, warrior, enchantress, or sorcerer.

BE GIVEN A NAME

In hierarchical packs, pack leaders or elders sometimes bestow names upon members. Often, a name indicates a wolf's ranking in the pack or his abilities, appearance, personality, or special talents.

GO ON A VISION QUEST

Some werewolf packs send their young teens out on vision quests to find their new names.

During periods of isolation and meditation, these initiate pack members receive visions of their futures as well as werewolf names.

NAMING CEREMONIES

Naming ceremonies can range from simple to elaborate. In large clans, members may also incorporate rites of passage. To have your own renaming ritual, invite a small number of your close werewolf and human friends to a place where you feel your werewolf essence strongly. It's best to perform this rite during a new or waxing crescent moon to signal the beginning of your werewolf journey. At these times you'll be more in control of your wolf nature.

NAMES FOR WOMEN

Adolpha Noble she-wolf (German)

Ailith Warrior (Old English)

Artemis Greek goddess of the hunt and of the moon

Chandra Moon (Sanskrit)

Circe Greek enchantress who changed people into animals with her spells

Luna Roman goddess of the moon

Luperca The she-wolf who nursed Romulus and Remus (Roman mythology)

Makoce Earth (Lakota)

Mielikki Finnish goddess of forests and hunting

Saida Huntress (Arabic)

Selene Greek goddess of the moon

Shamira Guardian (Hebrew)

Silvana Forest (derived from Latin)

Tamamo Name of an ancient kitsune (Japanese)

Tanith Phoenician goddess of the moon, stars, and love

Ulrica Power of the wolf (old German)

NAMES FOR MEN

Adalwolf Noble wolf (German)

Azim Protector (Arabic)

Bodulfr War wolf (Icelandic)

Chandrakant Beloved by the moon (Sanskrit)

Cuán Little wolf or little hound (Irish)

Fenris or Fenrir Mythical monster wolf (Norse mythology)

Freki One of Odin's wolves (Norse mythology)

Koray Ember moon (Turkish)

Lupin Wolflike (derived from Latin)

Lykos Wolf (Greek)

Mahigan Wolf (Algonquin)

Remus One of Rome's founders, who was raised by she-wolf Luperca

Romulus Brother of Remus and son of Luperca; cofounder of Rome

Sköll Treachery (the name of the wolf that chases the sun in Norse mythology)

Varg Wolf (Old Norse)

Whether you reside in a simple log cabin or a stately mansion, your den is your fortress, your refuge from the human world.

FIND YOUR
IDEAL DEN

Are you a dark, brooding werewolf who haunts a crumbling mansion or a modern wolf who lives in a swanky townhouse with a sweeping view of the city? Just as there are different types of werewolves, there are different ways they express themselves in their home decor. This quiz will help you ascertain the style that best suits your personality.

1 WHAT IS THE DOMICILE OF YOUR DREAMS?

A. A modern loft with a city view.
B. A boarded-up mansion with an overgrown garden and an imposing wrought-iron fence.
C. A little cottage surrounded by cherry trees and a fishpond.
D. A big place in the country where you can run wild.

2 HOW DO YOU ENTERTAIN AT HOME?

A. Hang out on your leather couch watching your huge, flat-screen TV.
B. Anyone who dares approach your house does so at his or her own risk.
C. Serve visitors tea and cookies in your garden.
D. Invite friends to join in for an hour of storytelling around the bonfire.

3 WHAT DO YOU EAT IN YOUR WOLF FORM?

A. Your fridge is stocked with fresh meat from the local butcher.
B. You eat whatever and whomever you like.
C. You eat lightly, taking only what nature provides—although you won't say no to bubble tea.
D. You like to hunt your own meat.

4 HOW DO YOU LIKE TO DRESS?

A. You're known for your stylish and chic outfits.
B. It's not an issue since you spend most of your time in wolf form.
C. A kimono or a pretty little dress does the trick just fine!
D. Something casual and sporty that allows for utmost maneuverability.

5 How Well Do You Tolerate Humans?

A. You crave urban excitement, so you've learned to deal with them.

B. The farther away you can keep the meddlesome scoundrels, the better—until you get hungry.

C. You often invite the ones you trust over for quaint parties.

D. You like them well enough, but you need a place where you can be alone sometimes too.

6 What Sort of Gathering Suits You Best?

A. Getting together with friends at a loud club or trendy restaurant.

B. A full-moon rampage with other like-minded werewolves.

C. A lovely night spent gazing at your moon pool.

D. Running through the woods with your family and friends.

IF YOUR ANSWERS ARE:

MOSTLY A's Your style is city werewolf. You like being at the center of everything hip and happening. Even if you don't live in a big city, you can still look the part by choosing modern, minimalist pieces in neutral colors and accenting them with a few dramatic accessories.

MOSTLY B's Your style is hungry wolf. You're more than a little dangerous, as your creepy, haunted abode attests. Dark, antique furnishings, twisted candelabras, and unsettling artifacts make your lair your own.

MOSTLY C's Your style is *kitsune*. Thoughtful and magical, you love exquisitely cultivated natural spaces, like tea gardens and fishponds. Your Japanese-style accessories give your home an air of peacefulness and utmost tranquility.

MOSTLY D's Your style is nature lover. A rustic cabin or lodge somewhere out in the woods would suit you fine. You naturally gravitate toward solid, comfortable furniture, simple wool blankets, and outdoor gear.

ULTIMATE
WOLF DEN

Now that you've identified your ideal decor, it's time to pad your den with a few finishing touches. No matter what your personal style, here are some accessories that any werewolf will appreciate. Remember, less is more! You don't want to end up breaking a bunch of nice furniture when you go through a violent transformation.

Floor Pillows
Wolves and people have one thing in common—they both like to curl up on a comfy pillow now and then. Some vampires might call it a dog bed, but they can bite you (no, really).

Mini Fridge
Keep some fresh raw meat around for those times when ravenous hunger strikes—hamburger meat is a convenient snack.

Secret Hideout

If you don't have the funds to commission a passage to a safe room, hang a curtain or put up a screen to make a secret space just for you. Hide there when stupid mortals come calling.

Moon Chart

If your transformation comes with the full moon, tracking moon phases is essential. A cool poster or painted mural of the lunar chart would look just right above your bed or a door.

Telescope

Star- and moon-gazing is an inspiring pastime, even if you're not a werewolf. Plus, you can use your scope to spot any angry citizens or vampires headed your way.

Teapot

Are you seeing an herbalist for help with those wolfy moods? Fix your tea in a teapot—no fancy china for you!

LYCANTHROPIC
LANDSCAPING

As a wolf, you naturally spend a good portion of your time outdoors. But even when you're in human form, your deep connection to the earth will make you long to commune with nature. Maybe you spend time hiking or in the park, but you can also create a little haven just for yourself—even if it's just in your own backyard.

GREEN SCREEN

Create a summer den for yourself by planting some fast-growing bamboo. You can hide away in your secret arbor and contemplate your next adventure. You might also get really doglike and dig out a cool, shady spot under a tree or tall hedge where you can doze lazily on a hot day. You know, like all dogs love to do.

HABITAT FOR WILDLIFE

Invite wildlife—from bees and birds, to squirrels and even bigger animals—into your garden by creating a backyard habitat. Provide food, cover, and water, and then sit back and wait to see who shows up. With a little planning, you can invite nature into any outdoor space, whether you have an apartment balcony or a rolling country estate. Plus, if you get hungry, you can always eat your little guests for snacks.

SUPERSPOOKY STYLE

Flowers that bloom at night make a cool and slightly creepy addition to any garden. Evening primrose, Casablanca lilies, angel's trumpet, nicotiana, and four o'clock flowers are just a small sample of the many spooky nighttime bloomers available. You might also want to plant lots of other white and yellow flowers to reflect and enhance the moon's glow.

REFLECTING POOLS

A fishpond or pool that reflects the moonlight is a perfect addition to any outdoor setting. At night, use this as a tranquil spot for meditation or just for contemplative moon-gazing. If you're a *kitsune*—bonus! You can eat the fish. *Kitsune* also enjoy cherry trees. At least buy some pretty flowering branches from a florist.

FRIENDLY FIREFLIES

Attract these bugs to your yard for a vivid nighttime display. For best results, don't use chemicals on your lawn or other plants, leave some high grass or shrubbery for them to rest in, and reduce artificial lighting.

WHITE STATUES

Place white statues throughout your garden or around your pond. They'll glow subtly and eerily under the moonlight. A statue of Artemis, the ethereal Greek goddess of the hunt, honors your savage side.

A COMFORTABLE SEAT

Whether you're watching the wildlife in your yard or gazing at the night sky, you'll need a comfy place to sit and take it all in. Try a wrought-iron seat with a cozy cushion, a roughly hewn bench, or an indoor-outdoor dog bed.

OTHER
WERECREATURES

Shapeshifters lurk in every corner of the world—and while werewolves are rightly the most famous of the lot, they aren't the only ones out there. Here are a few you may encounter in your travels.

WERECATS

Sly and cunning, werecats are aloof creatures known for their elegance and independence. Most werecats are witches who use their magic to shapeshift. This mysterious allure makes them extremely popular in books and movies.

WEREDOGS

Humans who turn into domesticated dogs are known as cyanthropes. Although they don't get the respect (or the notoriety) that werewolves do, their loyalty, good nature, and protective instincts make cyanthropy a popular option for shapeshifters who don't wish to appear to others as fearful monsters.

WERETIGERS

Indigenous to many parts of Asia, weretigers are fearsome and proud predators. Local lore suggests that they are powerful sorcerers or human-eating beasts who acquired the power of shapeshifting by eating lots of humans.

WERERABBITS

These ravenous bunnies are rare, thankfully. Able to easily deplete a small town's vegetable gardens in a handful of nights, they are typically formed as the result of experimentation gone awry. For some reason, British inventors appear susceptible to transformation—like in *Wallace & Gromit: The Curse of the Were-Rabbit.*

WERECROWS

People who change shape into birds often pick the crow form. Werecrows that serve witches as messengers are wily, crafty, and untrustworthy. Some, however, forge mystical connections with humans. In rare cases, they have been known to help humans come back from the grave to avenge their own wrongful deaths.

WERELIONS

In certain parts of Africa, legends suggest that anyone with the power to shapeshift into lion form must be a king or a leader. Some claim that the lions of Tsavo—two people-eating lions who attacked builders of the Kenya-Uganda railroad at the end of the nineteenth century—were in fact werelions trying to stop colonial incursion.

WEREJAGUARS

Ancient Aztec warriors who dressed in jaguar skins before going into battle were among the first known werejaguars. These large, stately cats with their beautiful spotted coats are also a favorite host choice for shapeshifting shamans and *nahuals.*

WEREFOXES

Seemingly cute and cuddly, werefoxes are the unlikely tricksters of the werecreatures set. These animals are notorious for their stealthy and mischievous ways—look out!

IT'S A WILD
WEREWOLF PARTY

Feeling like a party animal? Invite your friends over for a night they'll never forget. Whether you party indoors or outside, you'll have a howling good time with these ideas and decorating tips.

INDOOR CAVE PARTY

Everyone knows that whenever awesome things happen, they happen first underground. Transforming your room into a cave will thrill and impress your wolfy friends and guarantee a superspooky party! Here's what you will need.

🐾 Tack burlap or other textured brown fabric onto your walls and ceiling to create your cave's rock-like interior.

🐾 Costume and party stores often carry fake spiderwebs. Drape these around your cave for a creepy look.

🐾 Litter your spiderwebs with black plastic spiders. If you can find spiders that glow in the dark, even better!

🐾 Put a black lightbulb in your light fixture. It will make any glow-in-the-dark critters emit an eerie luminosity.

No cave is complete without some animal pelts used as rugs. Buying fake animal-print fur and cutting it into shapes will do the trick.

Get out the cardboard and pale yellow paint and make yourself a giant full moon. Put it up within view of the mouth of your cave. For extra atmosphere, illuminate it with a bright light. Glow-in-the-dark paint is a bonus.

Search toy stores for rubber bats to hang from the roof of your cave! And, of course, use glow-in-the-dark bats if possible—they'll shine beautifully in your black light.

OUTDOOR BONFIRE PARTY

With adult supervision and guidance, you can have a really fun full-moon campfire gathering or bonfire beach party. Here's what to bring.

First off, you'll need some firewood and kindling for your fire. Make sure your parents or other adults handle this aspect of your party.

Bring blankets to sit on around your bonfire, as well as some extras to keep any human friends warm and snuggly.

Depending on where you live, even summer nights can get chilly. Don't forget to bring a warm jacket if you will be staying in human form for the festivities.

Make sure you have some hot chocolate and sweet treats, such as tasty moon-shaped cookies. Or you could pack some marinated meat to grill for kebabs—if you take on your wolf form, you can just gulp them down raw.

Take along a drum, an acoustic guitar, a fiddle, or any instruments you might have. Play some music around the fire for your friends to howl along with.

Bring stories to share about your ancestors, your wild werewolf adventures, and any other thrilling escapades.

WEREWOLF
PARTY RECIPES

Y ou've decided what sort of werewolf party to have—but what do you feed your guests? Human friends will need more than raw meat. Here are some werewolf-inspired treats that everyone will enjoy.

MOON-SHAPED COOKIES

Find a cookie cutter in the shape of a crescent moon and make some moon cookies. You can follow your favorite homemade recipe or buy some premade cookie dough. If you don't have a rolling pin, a tall water glass will do the trick. Be sure to use plenty of flour when rolling out the dough so it doesn't stick to the counter surface, rolling pin, or cookie cutters. Coat the cookies in powdered sugar to give them a nice white glow. Making a series, from crescent to full moon, and arranging them on a dark-colored platter would be a fun project.

MIDNIGHT MOON CAKE

Use a round baking pan for this frighteningly delicious chocolate cake. Buy a packaged dark chocolate cake mix or use your favorite recipe. (Note: If the recipe calls for water, substitute black coffee for some of the water. If the recipe calls for milk, then add one shot of espresso—or a few tablespoons of very strong coffee—to the milk.) Bake the cake according to instructions, let it cool, and then top it with pale cream-cheese frosting to evoke the moon. You can buy premade frosting, but it is supereasy to make. Mix together 16 ounces (452 g) of cream cheese, ½ cup (115 g) of butter, 2 cups (260 g) of sifted confectioners' sugar, and a teaspoon of vanilla, using a hand mixer, until creamy and smooth.

CAMPFIRE TREATS

If you're having an outdoor bonfire party, be sure to bring along some marshmallows, hot chocolate mix, and hot water (or warm milk) in a large thermos to help you stay cozy all night. Roast marshmallows on sticks over the fire and enjoy a gooey treat.

THRILL OF THE GRILL

If your parents will supervise, you can throw a wolf-style barbecue. For human guests, grill hamburgers, hot dogs, sausages, or other meats. Or, for a change of pace, serve steak kebabs (you'll need to soak the skewers in water first so they don't char). If you have vegetarian friends, don't forget to grill veggie dogs, tofu, and vegetables.

THE PERFECT STEAK

Most werewolves think of the perfect steak as one they just ripped from a deer's flank. For more sophisticated tastes (and for squeamish humans), here's the ultimate meaty treat. Start with high-quality cuts of steak like filet mignon. Let them sit at room temperature for a few minutes, place them on the grill, cover, and flip them when one side starts to show grill marks. When the second side has marks, take it off the fire and let it sit for a few minutes to seal in the juices. If it's too rare (what kind of werewolf are you?), throw it back on for a minute or two.

WEREWOLF BANDS

ome bands evoke a lycanthropic atmosphere with a gritty singing style or reference wolfy terms just because they are enthusiasts. Either way, your supersensitive hearing is in for a treat.

Guitar Wolf
This entertaining Japanese trio is a garage punk band whose members all appeared in the crazy and raucous zombie film *Wild Zero*. So, they know their supernatural beasties!

Wolfsheim
This German dark-wave band makes highly danceable music that's perfect for grinding the night away at werewolf nightclubs.

Wolfmother
Australia's wolfiest hard-rock band has been compared to everyone from Black Sabbath to (hmmmm . . .) Steppenwolf.

Wolf Eyes
This American post-industrial noise band revels in horrorcore's staple themes like violent death. Their delightful tunes will suit werewolves who like their music dark and noisy.

Los Lobos
Los Angeles–based Chicano rockers, Los Lobos sing about wolves, full moons, and other wolfy topics in a style that mixes Tex-Mex, norteño, and roots rock.

Wolf Parade
Werewolves looking for catchy dance rock should definitely check out these indie rockers from Montreal.

Queen Ida
This Louisiana-born musician is a zydeco legend. With elements of blues, R&B, and Cajun, her music is a backwoods werewolf's dream.

Sea Wolf
The indie folk-rock band Sea Wolf contributed "The Violet Hour" to the *New Moon* soundtrack.

Devendra Banhart
An American singer-songwriter, Devendra Banhart is known for his freak-folk compositions and trippy lyrics. Plus, the facial hair is a dead giveaway that he has lycanthropic tendencies.

Steppenwolf
If there's a werewolf music hall of fame, you know it includes "Born to Be Wild," a late 1960s hit by this Canadian-American hard-rock group.

Gene the Werewolf
Fang-in-cheek fun, Pittsburgh-based Gene the Werewolf delivers feel-good party rock.

The Birthday Party
Nick Cave's band before the Bad Seeds, this Australian outfit creates gothic post-punk compositions that excel in setting a dark mood.

Howlin' Wolf
An American blues singer known for his raw voice and ripping blues style, Howlin' Wolf is a cornerstone of werewolf blues-rock.

SONGS TO MAKE YOU
HOWL

All werewolves need some killer music for the soundtracks of their lives—it can soothe you during a rough transformation or add atmosphere to your memories. Here are some songs to listen to while you're wolfing around.

PROWLING FOR ADVENTURE

Deep in the Woods The Birthday Party

The Hungry Wolf X

Run Through the Jungle The Gun Club

Run with the Wolves The Prodigy

Jumpin' at the Woodside Count Basie

Born to Be Wild Guitar Wolf

New Moon Rising Wolfmother

Killer Wolf Danzig

ON THE HUNT

HUNGRY LIKE THE WOLF
Duran Duran

A WOLF AT THE DOOR Radiohead

BARK AT THE MOON Ozzy Osbourne

BAD MOON RISING
Creedence Clearwater Revival

WOLF LIKE ME TV on the Radio

OF WOLF AND MAN Metallica

WEREWOLF LOVE

Blue Moon Elvis Presley

Moondance Van Morrison

Li'l Red Riding Hood
Sam the Sham and the Pharaohs

Moon over Bourbon Street Sting

Werewolf Cat Power

Care for You Wolfsheim

She Wolf Shakira

Wolf Moon Type O Negative

You're a Wolf Sea Wolf

I Wanna Be Your Dog
Iggy Pop

HANGING WITH YOUR PACK

Werewolves of London
Warren Zevon

Suburbia
Pet Shop Boys

Who's Afraid of the Big Bad Wolf
B5

Ain't Gonna Be Your
Dog No More
Howlin' Wolf

Will the Wolf Survive?
Los Lobos

I Was a Teenage Werewolf
The Cramps

PROWL THESE VACATION
HOT SPOTS

Whether you're thinking about expanding your territory or simply interested in hunting down some wild new experiences, here are some must-see sites for the globe-trotting werewolf.

THE HIMALAYAS

While you're soaking in the majesty of this mighty mountain range, which covers parts of India, China, Tibet, Bhutan, and Nepal, keep an ear cocked for the howl of a Tibetan wolf. This Asian subspecies of the gray wolf—the most prominent predator in Tibet—is feared and revered for its hunting abilities.

EPHESUS, TURKEY

Rediscovered in 1869 by British archaeologists, the Temple of Artemis in Ephesus (just outside modern-day Selçuk) was one of the seven most awe-inspiring wonders of the ancient world. Although fragments of the temple are all that remain today, this is a site of powerful energy for the mystically inclined—especially for werewolves, with their connection to the moon goddess (who is also the goddess of hunters).

THE AMERICAN SOUTH

The swampy backwoods areas of the American South are prime spots for hanging out with local *loups-garous*. Groups of French werewolves settled in the Louisiana Territory centuries ago, and now you can find them on Bourbon Street in New Orleans, navigating the Florida Everglades, or playing zydeco in juke joints anywhere from Louisiana to East Texas. Head to New Orleans for the annual jazz festival, and you're sure to see a few werewolves getting down.

THE BLACK FOREST

Werewolf lore runs deep in Germany. Travel to the fabled Black Forest in the southwestern part of Germany to see the birthplace of many fairy tales. While you're there, sample some of the region's Black Forest ham. Even though you won't be gobbling up woodcutters and children in this day and age, you'll still eat well.

ELKHORN, WISCONSIN

This rural town is the place where the Wisconsin werewolf known as the Beast of Bray Road was first spotted in the 1980s. Described as large, hairy, and able to walk on two legs, this particular cryptozoological mystery might be an American wolfman. Although movies and books have explored the story, you may find the truth here.

TRUJILLO, PERU

View the remains of spectacular temples from Peru's ancient Moche culture. The Huaca de la Luna, or Moon Temple, is a series of overlapping tombs decorated with haunting murals that hint at mysterious sacrificial rites.

KOH SAMUI, THAILAND

The sun-kissed beaches of this popular Thai island are the site of legendary full-moon parties that attract thousands of revelers. You'll meet werewolves from all over the world—get ready to dance until daylight.

SEE THE WORLD OF
THE WOLF

Plot a course and explore your heritage, history, and ancestors. Here are some notable stops to make on your werewolf world tour.

YELLOWSTONE

This spectacular national park in Wyoming is the home to an extensive effort to reintroduce wolves into the ecosystem. Feel your wolf ancestry as you watch for wildlife including dangerous grizzly bears and tasty, tasty elk.

ROME

Visit Rome and see many tributes to Romulus and Remus, the mythological founders of Rome. The most famous statue of them shows the twin brothers suckling from their adoptive wolf mother. You can find it, among other treasures, in the Capitoline Museum.

LONDON

Prowl the underground of London and see where some of the bloodiest scenes in *An American Werewolf in London* took place. Visit Piccadilly Circus to view the site of the film's moving finale.

KYOTO

Statues of *kitsune* guard the entrances to the Fushimi Inari shrine in Kyoto. Come to pay your respects to Inari, a deity in the Shinto belief system, and leave an offering of rice, sake, or food. Your *kitsune* sisters will smile on you and may even lead you on a fun and frolicsome adventure.

SWEET
WEREWOLF RIDE

Yes, you love running around wild and free in your wolf form, but let's be honest—there's nothing werewolves like better than a car ride where they can stick their heads out the window.

THINGS TO DO FOR
MANY, MANY MOONS

As a werewolf, you've got speed, strength, and style to burn. Sure, it's fun to nose around in the woods, but there's a lot more to werewolf life! Here are some ideas for getting the most out of your lycanthropy and exploring your wild nature to its fullest—especially if you're one of the lucky wolves whose gifts include immortality.

1 SAVE THE WOLVES
In many places around the world, wolves are struggling for their survival. Dedicate yourself to the conservation of wolves and their habitats. Or buy land and create a wolf preserve of your own.

2 START YOUR OWN PACK
If you're ready to be a leader, strike out and find followers. Young werewolves who need someone to show them the ropes will be excited to join you.

3 LEARN TO RIDE A MOTORCYCLE
Start your own fierce pack of werewolf chopper riders! Bikers are hairy anyway, so no one is going to look twice if you transform unawares, and the helmet hides it all. Plus, everyone looks good in leather.

4 MAKE FRIENDS WITH A VAMPIRE
It's so crazy, it just might work. With your odd-couple friendship going strong, you just might start a detective agency, fight crime, or fall in love.

5 MAKE THE WORLD'S COOLEST PANIC ROOM
When you need to get away from it all, you might as well do it in style. Get a big-screen plasma TV, a meat locker, and more—it should all be secured, in case things get chaotic.

6 BUY A CATTLE RANCH
You and your friends will always have a large supply of food on a beef ranch. Plus, you'll be able to make sure your meat is top-quality. If you're successful, start selling to restaurants—just don't bite the waiters.

7 BECOME A SUPERHERO
Secretly fight the forces of evil. You can even wear a cape if you really want to! Your wolfy senses and superstrength will come in handy and do some good in the world.

8 VISIT THE GERMAN VILLAGE OF EPPRATH
This tiny village was the birthplace of Peter Stumpp, the infamous Werewolf of Bedburg, who was executed. Learn about your heritage and thank your lucky stars you weren't wolfing around in the sixteenth century.

9 MAKE A CAREER OF PROTECTING HUMANS

With your superhuman senses and strength, you're a natural protector. You can join the police force or become a firefighter (you'll be able to sniff out fires before the alarm even goes off). With your tracking abilities, you'd make a great detective! Not the law enforcement type? What about being a forest ranger?

10 BECOME A FIERCE FASHION DESIGNER

Create stylish, rip-proof, stretchy outfits for the fashionista werewolf on the go. With the money you make, you can build the coolest werewolf hangout ever for yourself and your super-stylish pack.

11 STUDY THE WONDERS OF HERBAL MEDICINE

Maybe you'll discover a potion to help you and your kin take control of your transformations. At the least, you'll be able to brew your own herbal teas to help balance your moods and maybe even work a spell or two.

12 LEARN TO SNOWBOARD

Why? Because a werewolf on a snowboard looks awesome. Plus, most types of wolves love the snow, and your fur coat is better than any ski jacket for staying warm. Your extraordinary strength and balance and your natural lack of fear will enable you to shred like a champ.

13 VISIT JAPAN

Hang with a friendly *kitsune*. Learn their practices, rituals, and ways. If a *kitsune* respects you, you may even find you've made a lifelong magical friend.

14 CHECK OUT THE VOODOO SALONS OF NEW ORLEANS

You'll meet zombies, vampires, voodoo queens, and the odd *loup-garou* or two. Take in the Mardi Gras parade while you're at it.

15 JOIN AN ALPINE RESCUE TEAM

Those Saint Bernards have got nothing on you. With your thick winter coat and cold-resistant paws, you'll be a real lifesaver.

16 VISIT SCOTLAND

Not only was it the setting of the suspenseful werewolf movie *Dog Soldiers*; it's also the home of werewolves who run around in kilts. See how you look with a nice tartan over your fur.

17 MAKE FRIENDS WITH A GHOST

Every werewolf needs a connection to the spirit world. Cultivate your own friendship with the denizens of the other side. They can be very helpful when demons or vampires threaten.

18 TAKE UP ASTRONOMY

The moon is just one of many interesting heavenly bodies out there. As a werewolf, you're already in tune with the night skies—why not take the time to deepen your appreciation and knowledge?

19 RECORD YOUR HOWL

Listen to your wolf voice. Even better, make a recording of you and your wolf friends howling, put it to music, then release it to become werewolf pop stars.

20 Be a Collector

You could live for a long time. Why not profit by collecting art, memorabilia, or any other item that will increase in value over the years? Just stay away from silver.

21 Make Friends with Other Wereanimals

Use your tracking skills to locate those rare werelions or werehedgehogs. Though shapeshifters may look different on the outside, chances are you've got a lot in common.

22 Videotape Your Transformation

Set up a video camera in your room so you can see what you look like when you change shape. Share your movies—you might just become a YouTube sensation.

23 Buy Your Own Hunting Lodge

Make the coolest werewolf clubhouse ever! Find an old lodge in the middle of nowhere for monthly getaways. Run free in wolf form without fear of hurting anyone.

24 Try Pro Sports

Some lycanthropes find that their condition makes them amazing basketball players. With your power and speed, you might do well at football or track. Find out where your hidden talents lie.

25 Embark on a Movie Career

What movie director wouldn't want a real, live werewolf to star in his or her horror movie? Show the special-effects artists what transformation really looks like, and wow audiences at the same time.

26 Start a Nightclub

Werewolves are hungry for their own night spots. Stop slumming in vampire dives and create your very own werewolf club where you can book live bands and howl till dawn. When the moon is on the wane, you can invite sympatico humans in.

27 Find Inspiration on a Vision Quest

Get away from civilization for a while and go someplace you can meditate on your inner wolfiness. Whether you make a connection to a great wolf spirit or simply feel more at peace with yourself, you'll come back stronger and more focused. The deserts of the American Southwest and Australia's Outback are popular for such excursions.

28 Visit the Moon

View the lunar landscape up close by becoming a space tourist. Your hardy wolf physiology means you can handle space travel better than human astronauts. Will you stay transformed the whole time you're on the moon? Who knows? No werewolf has ever tried it before!

29 Write About Your Wolfy Adventures

Delight readers everywhere with fascinating tales of what a werewolf's life is really like. You can blog (remember: on the Internet, no one knows you're a wolf!), or even publish your account as "fiction." Your fans will love the realistic details in your writing.

30 Get a Guitar

Learn to play the blues. You've got so much soul in that furry body of yours, maybe one day you'll be another Howlin' Wolf.

MOONLIGHT MASTERY

Now that you've learned the fine arts of living stylishly as a werewolf, it's time to extend your mastery by discovering some of lycanthropy's deepest secrets. Delve into the hidden history of werewolfism by studying the paw prints your ancestors have left behind in global myths and legends.

In this chapter you'll also learn about real people who have been convicted of werewolfism, as well as the superstitions and lore surrounding your heritage and history. As you grow in power and knowledge, turn your wild gaze to the visions of storytellers: the writers and filmmakers who struggle to depict your life's glory—and gore—within the pages of books or the confines of a movie screen.

There's much for you to learn from humanity's intense fears—and its glorious celebrations—of your kind. Mastery of this information brings you closer to the ideal harmony between your human and animal sides. Read on, feast deeply, and then venture forth, proud of your true essence—strong, unmatched . . . werewolf.

TEST YOUR WEREWOLF
KNOWLEDGE

When it comes to knowing the secrets of your breed, are you an alpha or a clueless cub? Take this quiz to find out what areas of study will help make your werewolf mastery more than fur-deep.

1. IN ANCIENT JAPAN, WHAT DID GRAIN FARMERS DO TO HONOR WOLVES?
A. Hung silver wolf talismans in trees.
B. Left food offerings near their dens.
C. Created shrines dedicated to them.

2. WHAT HISTORICAL FIGURE WAS TRIED AS A WEREWOLF?
A. Peter Stumpp.
B. Caligula.
C. Queen Victoria.

3. WHEN WAS THE FIRST WEREWOLF FILM MADE?
A. 1951.
B. 1913.
C. 1922.

4. WHAT PLANTS ARE KNOWN TO HELP REPRESS WEREWOLFERY?
A. Wolfsbane.
B. Poppy flower.
C. Mistletoe.

5. WHICH GODDESS WAS KNOWN FOR TURNING PEOPLE INTO ANIMALS?
A. Ishtar.
B. Sekhmet.
C. Circe.

6. IN WHAT MOVIE OR TELEVISION SERIES DOES WEREWOLFISM APPEAR IN RESPONSE TO A THREAT?
A. *Buffy the Vampire Slayer*.
B. *Underworld*.
C. The Twilight saga.

7. A DIRE WOLF IS . . .
A. An extinct prehistoric wolf.
B. A wolf that preys on cattle and other livestock.
C. A popular drink at many werewolf watering holes.

8. WHAT MEDICAL ISSUE IS OFTEN CONFUSED WITH WEREWOLFISM?
A. Hypertrichosis.
B. Clinical lycanthropy.
C. Porphyria.

9 WHAT WEREWOLF FILM WON AN ACADEMY AWARD FOR BEST MAKEUP?

A. *Twilight: New Moon.*
B. *An American Werewolf in London.*
C. *Wolf.*

10 WHAT IS *SHE-WOLF OF LONDON*?

A. A little-known book by *White Fang* author Jack London.
B. The name of a luxury yacht owned by Madonna.
C. A TV show featuring an attractive female werewolf.

ANSWER KEY

1 All are correct. Grain farmers in ancient Japan honored wolves, believing them capable of granting humans protection and wishes.

2 A. Peter Stumpp was accused of werewolfism, tried, tortured, and executed in 1589.

3 B. *The Werewolf* was a short silent film that featured a Native American werewolf. Fire unfortunately destroyed all copies in 1924.

4 All are correct. All three plants are known to keep werewolves from transforming into their wolf state, but the correct dosage is essential.

5 C. This Greek enchantress amused herself by turning people into various types of animals, including, of course, wolves.

6 C. In the Twilight series, the appearance of vampires causes certain members of the Quileute tribe to become werewolves.

7 A. The aptly named (due to its fearsome size) dire wolf roamed North and South America during the Middle to Late Pleistocene Era.

8 All are correct. However, clinical lycanthropy is the only condition that causes a person to believe he or she actually is a werewolf.

9 B. The special effects and makeup for this 1981 film were groundbreaking for their time.

10 C. This short-lived TV show centered on an American graduate student turned werewolf.

SCORING

Give yourself one point for each correct answer.

0–3 What's the matter, were you raised by wolves? Stop sniffing fire hydrants and start educating yourself.

4–7 Better, but you haven't made alpha yet. Further study is required.

8–10 We bow in submission before you, leader. Your wolf pack awaits your orders.

REAL-LIFE
WEREWOLVES

These infamous names date from pre–Enlightenment Europe, when waves of werewolf hysteria swept the land. While the Inquisition prowled for anyone suspected of witchcraft or werewolfery, scores of people were accused, and often tortured and executed. Herewith are tales of some of the darkest moments in werewolf history.

PETER STUMPP

This sixteenth-century German man confessed to werewolfism after extensive torture. Saying the devil gave him a magic belt that enabled his transformations, Stumpp claimed to have hunted and eaten several people while in wolf form. His execution in 1589 was so legendary that he, the so-called Werewolf of Bedburg, would live on in many fictional creations.

THE WOLF OF ANSBACH

In 1685, the citizens of Ansbach (a small town in what is now Germany) believed the savage wolf plaguing their town to be a reincarnation of their former mayor. This cruel official was so hated that, when the wolf was eventually captured and killed, the townsfolk dressed it up in human clothing, a mask, and a wig, and hung up its carcass for public display.

GILLES GARNIER

Also known by his nom de loup, the "Werewolf of Dole," this sixteenth-century Frenchman was burned at the stake in 1573 after confessing to crimes of lycanthropy and witchcraft. His string of cannibalistic murders may have been the result of a deranged mind—or of the powerful ointment he claimed helped him transform.

THE GANDILLONS

In 1598, this family from Burgundy, France, was prosecuted and put to death by demonologist Henri Boguet. They confessed under torture to receiving a magic salve and wolfskin clothing from the devil. Their lurid statements included tales of a witches' Sabbath attended entirely by werewolves, and thereby sealed their doom.

JEAN GRENIER

If you believe the account of this disturbed French teenager, Satan was still distributing magical skin cream and fur coats in France five years after the execution of the Gandillons. In 1603, Jean Grenier confessed to a series of over-the-top escapades that even prosecutors suspected were lies. Four hundred years too early for reality TV, this poor attention-hound lived out the rest of his days in a monastery.

THE BEAST OF GÉVAUDAN

Cryptozoologists suspect that wolf-dog hybrids or Asian hyenas were responsible for savage attacks on humans and livestock that took place in the countryside of Gévaudan, France, in the eighteenth century. Although we might never know the truth about the beasts, their dark legend has inspired writers and filmmakers.

"He soon emerged in the form of a wolf"

THE WERE-WOLVES.

THEY GET MISTAKEN FOR WEREWOLVES
ALL THE TIME

Believe it or not, it's not always easy to tell who the real werewolves are in a furry, bloodthirsty crowd. Various medical disorders, psychiatric symptoms, and even spiritual practices can mimic the supernatural condition of werewolfery. A fail-safe way to identify true werewolves is by their power to change physically—accept no substitutes.

HYPERTRICHOSIS

This rare genetic mutation results in excessive hair growth, sometimes over the entire body and face. People with hypertrichosis can grow a coat of hair that looks so much like fur, they've often been mistaken for werewolves. In the past, people who suffered from this condition often ended up on display in sideshow attractions as either wolfmen or bearded ladies. Some grew so tired of being feared and ostracized that they chose to go all the way, becoming infected and enjoying happy lives as members of a pack.

CLINICAL LYCANTHROPY

When it comes to this psychiatric disorder, the werewolf is all in the sufferer's head. People with clinical lycanthropy truly believe that they have transformed into an animal. But, although they exhibit episodes of animal-like behavior, such as growling or running around on all fours, they remain in human form. To the psychiatrists treating these patients, the transformations are nothing more than delusions.

THERIANTHROPY

Now these people really embrace their animal side. Therianthropes (or therians, for short) truly believe that they can transform spiritually into animals. Therianthropes may look human on the outside, but on the inside, their souls howl with animal spirits. Certain therians experience such a strong connection to a particular animal that they believe it represents their true identity and that their human form is the false one.

PORPHYRIA

A potentially fatal disease, porphyria can cause excessive hair growth, skin discoloration, an aversion to sunlight, and sometimes severe stomach pain along with mental disturbances. This terrible affliction has sometimes been suggested as a possible origin of werewolf and vampire "myths." Myths? Bah! We all know werewolves and vampires actually exist!

FERAL CHILDREN

Myth and literature abound with tales of orphaned or abandoned children who were literally raised by wolves. Perhaps the most famous examples are Romulus and Remus, the legendary twin brothers who were suckled by a she-wolf and later founded Rome. Other cases of wild children have been reported through the ages, but these strange and fascinating humans are usually not werewolves—just people with really, really bad table manners.

LEGENDS
AND LORE

Werewolves have been running wild in folklore, legend, and myth around the world for thousands of years. Here is some of the frightful and fanciful lore that their kind have inspired.

SCOTTISH TALES

If wolves disturbed the dead, would the corpses come back to life as werewolves? Maybe that possibility isn't high on most people's list of fears, but long ago in Sutherland, Scotland, it was. Villagers were so worried about the wolves who scavenged human graves that they resorted to burying their dead on the Isle of Handa—a remote, rocky outcropping surrounded by water.

IRISH LORE

Shapeshifters have long haunted the Emerald Isle. In medieval times, the race of Laighne Faelaidh were thought capable of changing themselves into wolves to kill cattle. Another shapeshifter of Irish legend was the Morrígan, also known as the Phantom Queen. This mythic goddess was said to have the ability to shift form into a wolf, a raven, or any other creature. According to yet another medieval tale, a priest traveling in Ireland encountered a wolf who spoke to him in human speech, much to his surprise. It turned out that the poor creature (once human) and his wife had been condemned to live as wolves for a period of seven years.

GREEK MYTHOLOGY

Classical literature is filled with dark tales of shapeshifting and metamorphosis. In one of the most famous of these myths, a disguised Zeus visited the court of the Arcadian king, Lycaon. The ultimate bad host, Lycaon tried to serve Zeus a dish of child's flesh for dinner. Rather predictably, this little trick did not turn out well. Zeus turned Lycaon into a wolf as punishment and destroyed the palace for good measure.

NORSE LEGENDS

No one can accuse the Vikings of sugarcoating their stories. Norse mythology is full of terrifying wolves like Fenrir (the son of shapeshifter Loki and giantess Angerboda), who is destined to bring about the end of the world. This warrior culture revered and desired prowess in battle so much that fighters turned to shapeshifting to give them a lethal edge. The fearsome Norse warriors called berserkers dressed in animal skins for battle. By "going berserk," they aimed to channel animal savagery and resistance to pain. Those warriors who eventually turned into werewolves were known as Úlfhednar.

CHINESE LEGENDS

Many Eastern tales celebrate dog-headed men as mystical creatures with noble intentions and great power. Others mention half-man, half-animal beings simply as intriguing, exotic curiosities found in remote places. According to one tale, the hero Fu Hsi created a dog-headed race after a destructive flood. And *The Liang Shu* (a history of the Liang Dynasty) describes a similar race that was believed to live east of a mythical country known as Fusang.

EGYPTIAN DEITIES

Ancient Egypt's Wepwawet is a deity with the body of a man and the head of a wolf. Often depicted as a soldier carrying a weapon, he goes by the title, "Opener of Ways," meaning that he opens the way to the underworld. While Anubis, the jackal-headed god, casts judgment in the underworld, Wepwawet seems to focus

on getting souls down there in the first place. The pharaohs used his image to symbolize their victories in battle. He was also associated with the city of Lycopolis, which in Greek means "city of wolves."

NATIVE AMERICAN TALES

Wolves and shapeshifters are a staple of many traditional Native American stories. Wolves figure prominently in the traditions of hunting cultures, particularly near the Arctic, where Inuit lore tells of Amarok, a giant wolf. Another wolf being, the Waheela, was said to live in the far north. Ojibwa legends tell of people who can turn into wolves. And in some Shoshone tales, wolves are protectors of the people. Some tribes may have practiced secret rituals involving the wearing of skins, intended to give participants the abilities and powers of animals. But for the Navajo, at least, shapeshifting and skinwalking were the result of evil practices and witchcraft.

ROMAN WRITINGS

Werewolves existed in ancient Rome, at least according to noted writers such as Petronius. In his ribald work *The Satyricon*, a young soldier is turned into a wolf after he desecrates a grave. And Ovid's *Metamorphoses* is a catalog of shapeshifting in the form of an epic poem.

STORIES FROM BRITTANY

Medieval lore from Brittany, France, gave rise to many legends about werewolves, some of them surprisingly sympathetic. For instance, in the tale of Melion, a knight who served King Arthur changes into a wolf to hunt for food for his wife. Indeed, she helps him change, using a magical ring, and then runs off with another man. It takes intervention from the great Arthur himself to return Melion to human form, and the story ends happily—a rarity for misunderstood medieval werewolves.

EUROPEAN ACCOUNTS

Werewolves received some of their worst press during the early Middle Ages in Europe. Lacking modern knowledge of genetics and infectious disease, people dreamed up superstitious and depressing explanations for werewolfism. Sadly, many thought werewolves were possessed by or followers of demons. Interestingly, they believed that the devil had the power to turn people into werewolves—but that saints did as well. Saint Patrick was thought to have turned a Welsh king into a werewolf for committing an offense against God. Saint Natalia was also said to have forced an Irish clan to turn into wolves.

EASTERN REPORTS

The Kashub people, of what is today Poland, believed that children born with a caul—a membrane covering the face—would become werewolves. They also thought that birthmarks and a birthday of December 25th were signs of werewolfism. Also, certain cultures in some areas of Eastern Europe believed werewolves to be similar to vampires. In Serbia, the term *vulkodlak* was used to mean both "werewolf" and "vampire," as both creatures were thought to desecrate graves and suck blood.

A NATURAL HISTORY OF THE WOLF

Wolves are some of nature's most beautiful and majestic creatures. Plus, they're your close relatives! Read on to discover some of the more interesting facts about your wolf brothers and sisters.

ORIGINS

How far do your wolf genes go back? Some paleontologists speculate that wolves evolved in Eurasia some 800,000 years ago and crossed into North America via the Bering Land Bridge around 400,000 years later. In the New World, wolves competed with the now-extinct dire wolf, a taller, heavier pack hunter and scavenger. Some scientists believe that dogs evolved from wolves, diverging in relatively recent history—a mere 35,000 to 15,000 years ago. The wolf and its coyote cousins are part of the Canidae family, along with foxes, domestic dogs, and jackals. Get ready for some interesting family reunions.

PHYSICAL TRAITS

Wolves—like werewolves—range considerably in size. A typical gray wolf may weigh from 75 to 85 pounds (35–40 kg) and can stand 2 to 3 feet (60–90 cm) high at the shoulder. Some wolf specimens, however, have weighed more than 170 pounds (75 kg)! And there's a reason you're so sure-footed on snow: slight webbing between the toes, as well as relatively large feet, let wolves navigate snowy terrain. Special blood vessels in the paws also keep footpads from freezing.

FAMILY LIFE

Like their werewolf counterparts, most wolves live in packs centered around their parents. Pups may stay with the family pack for up to two years before moving out to start their own families (and almost never move back home after college). Wolves are usually monogamous, meaning they stay with one partner for life.

HUNTING

Wolves eat large mammals such as elk, bison, deer, and caribou, which they hunt in packs. Blame your wolfish side if you tend to binge eat—wolves typically eat about 3 to 10 pounds (1–5 kg) of meat at a time. If they've had a long gap between meals, they may wolf down 20 pounds (9 kg) of meat or more!

THE WOLF TODAY

Wolves are endangered in many places where they once roamed freely. In the United States, programs to reintroduce wolves are in place at Yellowstone National Park and along the U.S.–Mexico border. But wolves still suffer from habitat encroachment and human attack. Wolf sanctuaries—as well as programs that help to compensate livestock owners for any losses caused by wolves—offer hope for the future.

LOST

One pair of leather breeches, dropped somewhere near the northwest clearing in the central forest, last Friday (the night of the full moon). Nice quality, really want them back. May smell a little like wet dog (sorry about that!). If found, please return to:

Marcus von Wolfenburg
339 Shady Oaks Way
Wolverton

Reward!

Hey, Lycanthropes!

Are you tired of being persecuted by humans? Do people look at you funny when you eat raw meat in public? Need some new recipes for wolfsbane potion that don't taste like dog butt? Join the Lycanthropy Society. We meet every Wednesday at 7 p.m. in Farmer Stubbes's barn. Unless it's a full moon, of course.

ATTENTION!

Citizens of All and Sundry Villages Hereabouts!

Be warned that evidence has been found of Lycanthropic Acts most vile, including:

HUMANS CONSORTING WITH FOREST CREATURES

✠

HIDEOUS TRANSFORMATIONS

✠

DEVOURING OF LIVESTOCK

✠

MYSTERIOUS RITUALS

If you observe any suspicious activities, report them IMMEDIATELY to the proper authorities.

Do not attempt to apprehend a werewolf or other shapeshifter unless you are a trained monster hunter.

REWARD!

5,000 gold pieces for information leading to the capture of a proven lycanthrope

THE LITERARY
LYCANTHROPE

Sink your teeth into some juicy reads, and learn what mortals (and perhaps a few clandestine werewolves posing as innocent writers) have said about your kind. Many of these books give insight into how to live a happy, productive life as a member of both human and lycanthropic societies. Others are mainly good for inducing howls of laughter. A few may be too scary for preteen readers, so ask your parents' permission if you're at all unsure.

BISCLAVRET
Marie de France (twelfth century)

One of the first werewolf novels, this story will fill you with historical pride and gratitude for its positive portrayal of werewolves (so rare in the Middle Ages!). In it, Bisclavret, a French noble, vanishes mysteriously every three weeks to go werewolfing. While his wife is horrified and schemes against him, the king realizes that he is a noble, gentle wolf and helps to save him from her plots. In this story, we learn that some wolves can transform back only if they put on their original clothing—so find a good hiding place for those pants when you go wolfy!

DARKER THAN YOU THINK
Jack Williamson (1948)

This wide-ranging tale from the golden era of science fiction details the discovery of an ancient struggle between humans and shapeshifters. A rip-roaring tale ensues, as the werewolves are revealed to be living secretly among humans and awaiting the legendary Child of the Night, whom they believe will lead them to victory.

WOLF MOON
Charles de Lint (1988)

A werewolf character named Kern is the hero of this haunting, believable young-adult fantasy novel. Lonely and isolated due to his wolf nature, Kern searches from village to village, yearning for human companionship, but always fearing what might happen if he gets too close to someone. In an epic battle with a cruel hunter, he learns more about his nature and at last finds his own kind of peace.

BLOOD AND CHOCOLATE
Annette Curtis Klause (1997)

Werewolves known as *loups-garous* live quietly and secretly among humans in this romantic, fantastical alternate history for young adults. Blessed by the moon goddess Selene with the ability to shapeshift, the *loups-garous* are strong and brave, embracing their dual natures. When a young *loup-garou* falls for a human boy, she must choose between her nature and her heart. A 2007 film adaptation changed the story almost entirely.

HARRY POTTER SERIES
J. K. Rowling (1997–2007)

The wonderful, magical world of Harry Potter features werewolf characters both good and evil. On the side of the heroes stands Remus Lupin, a strong force for good. As a Hogwarts professor, he helps Harry learn the protective Patronus charm. After resigning that post, he is part of the re-formed Order of the Phoenix, guiding and supporting Potter. Sadly, savage, Voldemort-following Fenrir Greyback offers an evil counterbalance.

TWILIGHT SERIES
Stephanie Meyer (2005–2008)

Sure, most people think this iconic best-selling series is about vampires. But the millions of members of Team Jacob know that a true connoisseur reads these romantic rhapsodies for the werewolves. Noble, fearless guardians of humans (and historic enemies of vampires), shapeshifting members of the Quileute tribe transform to protect their land and the ones they love.

SHIVER
Maggie Stiefvater (2009)

The first novel in a young-adult series-to-be, this romantic tale of werewolf love and lore has won multiple awards for its storytelling and no-nonsense approach to werewolfery in a small American town. It tells of a young girl who is rescued by a yellow-eyed wolf as a child. Every winter as she grows older, she sees this wolf in the woods behind her home, gazing at her longingly. When she begins a romance with a handsome yellow-eyed boy, things start to get a little bit complicated.

RED RIDER'S HOOD
Neal Shusterman (2005)

This action-packed reimagining of the fairy tale *Little Red Riding Hood* begins when Red Rider, a sixteen-year-old boy, heads to his grandma's house in his bright-red Mustang to give her some "bread" (money). When a gang called the Wolves confronts him, things start to get hectic. It turns out that the gang members are werewolves, and the story takes exciting twists and turns. While the werewolves are the bad guys here (boo!), it's still an awesome ride.

WERELING SERIES
Stephen Cole (2005)

When teenage Tom Anderson wakes up after a life-threatening accident, he starts noticing that he's feeling . . . strange. And really craving red meat. Once he realizes that he has inadvertently hooked up with a family of werewolves, he and his shapeshifting love interest, Kate, go on the run, pursued by a pack that wants him dead. Over the course of three novels Tom and Kate battle forces of evil within and without, and search for a rumored cure for his werewolfism.

WOLF PACK SERIES
Edo Van Belkom (2005–2007)

This teen series of four books begins with a kindly forest ranger rescuing four orphaned wolf cubs in the Canadian wilderness. He and his wife soon discover that these are no ordinary wolves, and decide to take in the little werecubs and raise them as their own. The story jumps forward to the werewolves' teen years, and a fast-moving plot develops, revolving around evil scientists, school bullies, heartless loggers, and ever so much more.

GRAPHIC DEPICTIONS OF
WEREWOLFERY

With their dramatic transformations and fearsome appeal, werewolves are natural subjects for comics and graphic novels. Most of these books are intended for teen readers, but some may be too intense for younger werecritters. Please ask your parents for guidance if you have any doubts.

WEREWOLF!

Part of an ongoing series of graphic novels about supernatural creatures, this volume on werewolves takes readers to the once-happy town of Dreadsad, where an evil female vampire is terrorizing the populace. It's up to a brave werewolf to save the day.

THE WORLD OF DARKNESS

The eternal battle continues in the pages of this multivolume collection of several comics based on White Wolf's popular role-playing games, including *Vampire: The Masquerade* and, even better, *Werewolf: The Apocalypse: Black Furies*.

THE DREAM HUNTERS

Fantasy superstar Neil Gaiman's Sandman series is filled with mystical and wondrous beasts. In this installment, he retells a Japanese fable about a beautiful werefox who tempts a mortal man. Modern *kitsune* can learn a few tricks!

OZ: INTO THE WILD

Many werewolves who want to be accepted as members of society look to Oz, the sexy shapeshifter from *Buffy the Vampire Slayer*. In this graphic novel, our hero journeys around the globe learning to cope with his dual nature.

WOLF'S RAIN

This manga series, based on popular anime, follows the fortunes of a pack of wolves in a cold world. Forced to pass as humans in order to survive, they search for the "moon flower" that will allow them to find their true home.

HYPER POLICE

In this fast-paced anime series set in a far-future Japan, most of the population has become monsters. The central characters are a trio of shapeshifters—a fox-girl, a cat-girl, and a male werewolf—who work as crime fighters.

LYCANTHROPE LEO

Although the main character of this manga series is a werelion, lycanthropes will enjoy this title for its sensitive treatment of werecreatures and its complex character development. Leo is neither a hero nor a villain, just an everyday shapeshifter trying to make sense of his crazy world.

STONEHAVEN: VOLUME 1

In this installment of the fantasy series, a kind country hick in search of his runaway daughter finds that city life isn't what it seems. The cast includes a centaur, elves, trolls, and werewolf bikers who are certainly up to no good.

YELLOW EYES, SILVER SCREEN

Werewolves, though misunderstood by humans in real life, have found enthusiastic fans on the silver screen. Those mesmerizing yellow eyes and silky fur were just made for movie stardom. Do be aware that many of the movies considered classics are not intended for younger viewers. Have your parents check the films out, and they will decide whether you should watch them.

THE CRAZE BEGINS

While not actually the first werewolf film ever made (that honor goes to *The Werewolf*, a 1913 movie about a Native American shapeshifter), 1941's *The Wolf Man*, starring Lon Chaney as a Welsh nobleman who is bitten by a werewolf, influenced the way werewolf characters would be portrayed in film for decades to come.

BACKPACKING ADVICE

An American Werewolf in London (1981) highlights the all-too-common and terrifying scenario in which college students go for a moonlit hike on the moors and are attacked by a bloodthirsty werewolf. David, the surviving student, struggles with his newfound dark and wild nature while cavorting around London in this bloody and humorous film.

WATCH OUT—VAMPIRES!

Werewolves and vampires have always had an uneasy relationship. Before *Underworld* (2003), that conflict had never been depicted in such a stylish way. This film, along with its prequel and sequel, depicts the battle between latex-clad vampires and leather-pants–wearing lycans, and it's more than just the fashions that are fierce. The series revels in centuries-old rivalries, forbidden vampire-lycan love affairs (which pretty much never go well), and a whole lot of creature-on-creature violence set to a pretty awesome goth-industrial soundtrack.

NO, REALLY—WATCH OUT

In *New Moon* (2009), the second installment of the record-breaking, blockbuster Twilight series, a pack of muscular werewolves may make some viewers question why they ever liked those pale, glittery vampires in the first place. This portion of the saga follows the growing friendship between series heroine Bella and her devoted werewolf friend, Jacob Black. Romance is in the air—or is it?

A RETURN TO THE MOORS

A 2010 remake of the amazing 1941 classic, *The Wolfman* stars Benicio Del Toro as a nobleman who, upon returning to his family's estate, falls victim to an ancient and transforming curse. On the trail of a mysterious beast who haunts the surrounding forest, our dark hero discovers an unexpected and somewhat unwelcome secret about himself. Want a hint? It involves a lush fur coat and big, scary teeth.

> Scene from *An American Werewolf in London* (1981)

FOR FURTHER
FULL-MOON VIEWING

IT'S A MONSTER PARTY

Sure, the title of this 1948 film is *Abbott & Costello Meet Frankenstein*, but the cinematic monsters they encounter also include Dracula and the Wolfman. Recently named as one of the top 100 funny films of all time, it features Lon Chaney returning to his iconic role as Wolfman Larry Talbot and serves as a loose sequel to that much less hilarious film.

HIGH-SCHOOL HERO

In 1985's *Teen Wolf*, Michael J. Fox plays an ordinary high-school student who seems destined to be disappointed—not only in love, but on the basketball court as well. Luckily for him, he starts manifesting lycanthropic tendencies. This is an encouraging movie for young werewolves to watch, because it shows a happy werewolf whose condition brings him popularity, mad sports skills, and true love. A TV adaptation is under way.

REBEL WITHOUT A CURE

Unlike the more upbeat *Teen Wolf*, 1957's *I Was a Teenage Werewolf* shows the tragic side of werewolfism. Rebellious teen Tony Rivers becomes a werewolf through hypnosis when he visits a therapist who happens to moonlight as a mad scientist. Mystery Science Theater 3000 first presented this film, now considered a camp classic, in 1997.

BEWARE OF BAD WOLVES

It's sad but true—some werewolves just can't control their antisocial (well, antihuman) natures. Many lycanthropes see 1981's *The Howling* as offensive to werewolves in that it portrays them as murderous bad guys. Still, this frightening and gory portrait of a TV journalist stalked by evil werewolves is a cautionary tale about letting the dark side within take control.

WOLFEN EVOLUTION

In the graphic horror film *Wolfen* (1981), based on best-selling author Whitley Strieber's novel, the "wolfen" creatures are not technically werewolves—they're wolves who are so highly evolved that, in this fictional world, they outrank humans on the food chain. It's a heartwarming tale of evolution gone right.

FRACTURED FAIRY TALES

The Company of Wolves (1984) takes place in a young girl named Rosaleen's fairy-tale dreams. In this fantastical take on Little Red Riding Hood's story, some of the most charming characters are revealed to be werewolves, as are some of the most dangerous. A good lesson in choosing your friends wisely!

BETTER LIVING AS LYCAN

Being bitten by a werewolf is a life-changing experience for the main character in the 1994 film *Wolf*. In his case, lycanthropy improves his job prospects and sense of well-being. Plus, he gets the weregirl.

HELP FROM FRIENDS

The highly successful 2001 French film *Le Pacte des Loups* (*Brotherhood of the Wolf*) depicts the eighteenth-century legend of the Beast of Gévaudan. It turns out that the fearsome beast has been mistreated at the hands of humans. Despite the beast's fear and anger, a loyal group of people support and protect it. And that's why you should never bite your friends.

> Scene from *Abbott & Costello Meet Frankenstein* (1948)

WHO HOLDS THE KEY?

A veritable who's who of monsters populates the exciting special-effects extravaganza *Van Helsing* (2004). In this rip-roaring (if not overly literary) adventure, the legendary vampire hunter Professor Abraham Van Helsing ventures to Transylvania with a character played by the star of *Underworld*, Kate Beckinsale, who really, really dislikes werewolves. An action-packed plot pits Frankenstein's monster, Dracula, and a wolfman against each other, but only a certain key werewolf transformation can save the day.

LOVE CONQUERS ALL

Loosely based on the best-selling teen novel, 2007's *Blood and Chocolate* follows a tense romance between a werewolf girl and the human boy she loves. The werewolves in this film (known by the French term *loups-garous*) generally try to hunt only the most evil of bad guys—and leave innocent humans alone—but that plan doesn't always work out as it should, and some wolves are more honorable than others. Still, the heroine is a consistently positive werewolf role model.

WEREWOLVES
ON TV

Luckily for modern wolf cubs, there is no lack of television shows featuring werewolves and other paranormal beings. On the small screen, werewolves and other shapeshifters range from scruffy underdogs to wolfishly attractive (and dangerous) creatures. Curl up on the couch with a juicy steak and enjoy.

BEING HUMAN

This series, originally made for British TV, and then remade in the US, features three room-mates—a ghost, a werewolf, and a vampire, just trying to lead normal lives. Hospital worker George, the werewolf, is kind of nerdy most of the time, but grows strangely attractive around the full moon. While the show has its humorous moments, the examinations of problems faced by supernatural creatures can be heartbreaking.

TEEN WOLF

This 2011 reboot proves that werewolves and high school athletes are, apparently, an irresistible combination. In this version, high-school outcast Scott McCall is bitten by a werewolf, and must learn to juggle all those basic high-school pressures . . . playing lacrosse, romancing a werewolf-killing hottie, and keeping his little secret under wraps.

BUFFY THE VAMPIRE SLAYER

Along with all the humor, epic battles, and teenage drama that make it great, *Buffy* also shows a lot of love to werewolves, and some helpful hints as well. Oz learned some medita-tion techniques in Tibet that he uses to keep his cool—maybe there's a tip or two here for you.

THE MUNSTERS

This classic television show featured an unusual suspernatural family: Lily, a vampire, and Her-man, a monster in the mold of Frankenstein, manage to beget Eddie, a little boy werewolf who gets into no end of mischief.

TRUE BLOOD

Although this HBO series is more concerned with vampires, *True Blood* does have its share of shapeshifters and a pivtoal werewolf character. The sleepy town of Bon Temps, Louisiana, is a sultry setting for a bit of intrigue, murder, and supernatural antics.

SHE-WOLF OF LONDON

A beautiful American graduate student travels to England to work with a professor of mythology. Sparks fly, and so does the fur, once a werewolf attacks her. She and the professor search for a cure while fighting various supernatural baddies.

SUPERNATURAL

Hunky brothers Sam and Dean Winchester travel around the United States tracking down super-natural beings just because they fear and misun-derstand them. The show is a helpful example of human mentality, tactics, and weaponry.

GAMES

FOR THE WHOLE PACK TO PLAY

Werewolf-themed role-playing games (RPGs) are a great way to test your lycanthropic skills or try on a new supernatural persona. Invite the whole pack over and see who gets eaten!

WEREWOLF: THE APOCALYPSE

This extremely popular RPG from White Wolf allows players to create werewolf characters based on the Garou race, as well as several other shapeshifting denizens of the supernatural realms. In the game's universe, werewolves are the heroes, defending the spirits of nature from those who would harm them. Game play and backstory are extremely intricate and inspired a book series.

TWILIGHT PRINCESS

In this Legend of Zelda game (for Nintendo GameCube and Wii), the main character, Link, must transform into a werewolf before he can save the world. While the player cannot initially control the transformation, this capability is unlocked partway through the game. In wolf form, Link retains his intelligence and does not become a ravening beast, to the joy of werewolf gamers everywhere.

TALES OF THE TEMPEST

An advanced race of werebeasts known as the Lycanths is forced to battle humans after Lycanth-created technology accidentally causes global devastation. This game for Nintendo DS allows for multiplayer quests and features the "beastman transformation system," which you can use to morph your character in battle.

THE SIMS 2: PETS

Players of this expansion pack for the megahit Sims game from Electronic Arts can transform into werewolves with just a little bit of effort. The lycanthropically inclined player must find a wolf with glowing eyes and establish a trusting friendship with it. Eventually, the wolf will bite the player, transforming him. WereSims have a range of special powers, including the ability to transform other players.

RAMPAGE

Based on a classic monster-themed arcade game, the *Total Destruction* installment of the Rampage game series is a release for Nintendo GameCube, Wii, and Sony PlayStation 2. It features Ralph the Werewolf in a battle for the title of King of the World. If you've ever wanted to stomp through cities like a werewolf Godzilla, putting the smack down on dinosaurs and super-rats, this is the game for you.

EQUINOX

This online RPG lets you play as a human, vampire, or werewolf character in a world based on the Twilight books. But, really, is there any doubt about which one to pick? (We didn't think so.) This is an all-ages game, but parental consent is required if you're under twelve.

A study of classic films is a
great way to learn tactics for
battling human foes.

> Scene from *Underworld: Evolution* (2006)

A WILD AND WONDERFUL
WORLD AWAITS

Both human and wolf live within you now. You have explored your dual nature and have come to a deeper understanding of the mysteries and wonders of the life lycanthropic. A glimmering dream dances before your yellow eyes—a vision of how you, a newly minted shapeshifter, can shape the world you live in. Will you take up the mantle of protector and champion of weaker creatures, running fearlessly through the forest, alert to both danger and opportunity? If you have read well and wisely, you will.

The wolf is a fearsome opponent but a noble and worthy ally. Armed with the knowledge you've gained from this book, you can rule the night with impunity. Find your pack, chart your course, and sink your teeth into the future. The world is yours. May the moon shine forever on your exploits.

FOR FURTHER STUDY

The wild bee reels from bough to bough
With his furry coat and his gauzy wing,
Now in a lily-cup, and now
Setting a jacinth bell a-swing,
In his wandering;
Sit closer love; it was here I trow
I made that vow,

Swore that two lives should be like one
As long as the sea-gull loves the sea,
As long as the sunflower sought the sun,—
It shall be, I said, for eternity
'Twixt you and me!

GLOSSARY

BROTHERHOOD OF LYCAON
For these beasts, wolf form is a punishment; they're serving time for their cannibalistic deeds.

CLINICAL LYCANTHROPY
A psychiatric disorder. Affected humans believe that they are animals but do not transform.

DEMON
Pure evil, a demon delights in tempting humans and werewolves to do bad deeds.

DESCENDANT OF FENRIR
These fierce Scandinavians may have inspired the legends of the Norse berserkers.

EGYPTIAN WEREJACKAL
Governed by the Egyptian god Anubis, these beasts with heads of jackals judge dead souls.

FAERIE
Though beautiful and alluring, some of these tricky sprites are downright malicious.

GUARDIAN WOLF
A noble and telepathic creature that uses his power only to protect his loved ones.

GHOST
The spirit of a deceased creature that is still in contact with the earthly realm.

HYPERTRICHOSIS
This genetic condition causes excessive hair growth and has caused numerous humans to be mistaken for werewolves.

THE INQUISITION
The goal of this crusade by the Catholic Church was to punish blasphemous citizens—including magical beings, and therefore werewolves.

JÉ-ROUGE
A mysterious werewolf spirit from Haiti that appears as a black dog or wisp of smoke. It is capable of possessing humans and has been known to steal village children.

KASHUBIAN SHAPESHIFTER
A childlike Eastern European werewolf, often mistaken for a faerie, that transforms at will.

KITSUNE
Female guardian werewolves from Japan, *kitsune* are charming, mischievous pranksters but are protective of those they trust.

LOUP-GAROU
The French term for "werewolf." Humans should beware of hungry *loups-garous* that may lurk beneath the Eiffel Tower during romantic, moonlit tours.

LUNAR CHART
Any werewolf, werewolf hunter, or fearful human should use a calendar of moon phases to be prepared for full moons.

LYCAN
This race of monstrous, immortal beasts is most feared among werewolves and has remained dedicated to war against vampires for centuries.

NAHUAL
Known and feared by humans, these magical Mexican werewolves are really more interested in mischief than serious battle.

NEURI
Ancient, cannibalistic, and shaggy, Neuri are quite a force to reckon with. Luckily, they only transform once a year.

NORSE BERSERKER

A warrior from Norway, considered to be as savage as an animal. Some werewolves take the form of a berserker when they transform, and others may be descendants of the Norse line.

PACK

A group of wolves that live and hunt as a family. Typically, a pack features a hierarchical clan structure and is led by the alpha wolf.

PORPHYRIA

A devastating affliction causing excess hair, discoloration, aversion to sunlight, mental disturbance, and stomach pain in humans. Some human skeptics have cited this disease in an attempt to explain away real lycanthropes.

SAFE ROOM

A secured den in which a werewolf may restrain himself during a full moon—an essential for any werewolf with a conscience.

SHAMAN

A priest or priestess who uses magic to heal, cast curses, and conjure hidden truth and who can be of assistance to supernatural beings.

SHAPESHIFTER

A creature that can physically transform to resemble other species.

SILVER

A metallic element, used as currency by humans, that is capable of causing werewolves agony.

SKINWALKER

Human shapeshifters of Navajo legend who have dark powers. Their ability to transform into any animal makes them extremely sneaky.

TEENAGE WOLF

A high-school student who uses lycanthropy to become a sports hero and popular date.

TELEPATHY

The ability to communicate psychically or read minds. Many werewolves have this power.

THERIANTHROPY

A term referring to spiritual connections between humans and animals or to creatures that live as part human and part animal.

TRANSFORMATION

The often painful process by which a human morphs into a supernatural being or an animal. In werewolves, transformation can involve rage, fever, excessive hair growth, and more.

VAMPIRE

These suave, bloodthirsty members of the undead world are typically werewolf enemies, but sometimes particular werewolves and vampires are able to get along.

VILKATAS

These mythical Baltic she-wolves transform at will into graceful wolf forms. They travel alone and are usually not a threat.

WITCH

With diverse magical powers and the ability to cast spells and concoct potions for just about anything, a witch can be a friend or a foe depending on her individual intent.

WOLFMAN

Often referred to as "classic" werewolves, these typically tortured humans undergo their beastly transformations involuntarily with the full moon. In the woods at night, you may hear them howl in regret after they kill.

WOLFSBANE

A toxic, flowering plant that can be used to repel werewolves if great care is taken in its usage; an excessive amount actually increases the chances of savage transformation.

HOWLING AT THE
SILVER SCREEN

The films reviewed on pages 120–123 are the true werewolfian classics. However, lycanthropes are such handsome dogs, they've starred or appeared in many notable flicks. Here are some more for that full-moon film festival you're planning. Be warned—some of them are rated for mature audiences, so check with a parent before viewing.

ALVIN AND THE CHIPMUNKS MEET THE WOLFMAN (2000)

Ever wanted to see those squeaky-voiced little varmints go snout-to-snout with a really hungry werewolf? Or even transform into one? This movie gives you that chance, along with all the songs and wacky mix-ups you could ask for.

CURSED (2005)

The team that brought you the horror film *Scream* returned with the thrilling tale of a werewolf loose in Los Angeles. Additional shapeshifting drama is introduced when a family's golden retriever is infected with the lycanthropic curse.

WALLACE & GROMIT: THE CURSE OF THE WERE-RABBIT (2005)

Apparently terror comes in every shape and size, including a massive Claymation bunny. Beloved team Wallace and Gromit are preparing for the big vegetable competition when an invention goes hilariously wrong, producing a big, hungry, and rather suspiciously familiar wererabbit. Hilarity ensues.

SKINWALKERS (2006)

Another movie that shows the deep, almost mythological bond between werewolves and motorcycles. In the *Skinwalkers* mythology, werewolves can be good or evil, and the two groups are in a constant state of battle. One dedicated young man will either bring an end to the werewolf curse or die trying.

NEVER CRY WEREWOLF (2008)

This movie was made for TV in Canada, but through the miracle of the Internet can now be viewed everywhere. It features Kevin Sorbo, a man whose very presence in the cast of a show promises a certain level of shameless cheesiness, and this movie does not disappoint on that front. A teen girl battles her suspiciously wolfy neighbor with awesome help from the man who once played Hercules.

WAR WOLVES (2009)

This movie originally aired on America's SyFy network. It follows the travails of several soldiers who return home from war in the Middle East only to slowly realize that they have become a pack of werewolves.

Тѣ́мъ молю́ся. Гдⷭ҇и Іи҃се свѣⷣте се...
мⷪ҇й, да не въ сꙋⷣъ ми свⷣꙋⷮ се...
сіѧ̀, за є́же недостойнꙋ ми бы́ти ...
ѡчище́ніе и ѡсвѧще́ніе дꙋши́ же и т...
во ѡбрꙋче́ніе бꙋдꙋщїѧ жи́зни и ц҃рт...
Мнѣ́ же, є́же прилѣплѧ́тися Бг҃ꙋ и ...
є́стъ, полага́ти во Гдⷭ҇ѣ ꙋпова́нїе ...
моегѡ̀. И па́ки: Ве́чери твоеѧ ...

BOOKS TO SINK YOUR
TEETH INTO

While you kill time in the safe room, why not curl up on your wolfy bed with a good read? Pages 116–117 of this book suggest the top werewolf reads, but there are loads more. Some of these books might be scary or have grown-up themes, so ask your alpha (and your parents) if they're appropriate for you to read.

GUILLAUME DE PALERME
Countess Yolande (1200)

A medieval French love poem that features a werewolf—how romantic can you get? In this heartwarming tale, a young foundling falls in love with the Roman emperor's daughter. Of course she is promised to a prince, but she and the wolf run away to live in the woods, disguised in bear skins. They are protected by the hero's werewolf cousin, and the whole story ends happily for a change.

THE STRANGE CASE OF DR. JEKYLL AND MR. HYDE
Robert Louis Stevenson (1886)

While Mr. Hyde is not technically a werewolf in this classic tale, many have speculated that the story is a veiled allegory about lycanthropy. Recent adaptations, like the BBC show *Jekyll*, have made the connection explicit.

OPERATION CHAOS
Poul Anderson (1971)

In this novel's fantastical alternate version of our world, magic is everywhere, and the hero is a werewolf who, with his witch companion, must stop a magical weapon. In the sequel, *Operation Luna* (published in 2000), our wolfish leading man must now thwart the forces of evil as they try to interfere with a crucial moon landing.

THE BLOODY CHAMBER
Angela Carter (1979)

The movie *The Company of Wolves* was based on a story from this collection that deals with folk- and fairy-tale themes—but from a modern viewpoint. Several stories in this volume involve werewolves or other shapeshifting animals.

THE MORTAL INSTRUMENTS
Cassandra Clare (2007–2011)

This series of books follows teen protagonists into a mystical, alternate New York, where demons and angels battle, faeries and vampires are everywhere, and werewolves are allies.

DARK GUARDIAN
Rachel Hawthorne (2009–2010)

This series of four books, intended for the young adult reader, focuses on the wild escapades of a group of werewolves known as shifters who live along the U.S.–Canada border. Plenty of romance, adventure, and danger play out as the series progresses.

INDEX

© 2012 Weldon Owen Inc.

415 Jackson Street
San Francisco, CA 94111
www.weldonowen.com

Weldon Owen is a division of

BONNIER

Library of Congress Control Number
on file with the publisher

ISBN 13: 978-1-61628-396-4
ISBN 10: 1-61628-396-3

10 9 8 7 6 5 4 3 2 1
2012 2013 2014

Printed by 1010 in Huizhou,
Guangdong, China

Originally published in hardcover
by Candlewick Press

weldon**owen**

President, CEO Terry Newell
VP, Publisher Roger Shaw
Executive Editor Mariah Bear
Senior Editor Lucie Parker
Project Editor Heather Mackey
Creative Director Kelly Booth
Designer and Illustrator Scott Erwert
Senior Designer Meghan Hildebrand
Production Director Chris Hemesath
Production Manager Michelle Duggan

Special thanks to Jacqueline Aaron, Ian Cannon,
Marianna Monaco, Katharine Moore, Gail Nelson-
Bonebrake, and Frances Reade.

Photography

All images courtesy of Shutterstock, with the following exceptions:
Alamy: 105–106, 111 **Bridgeman:** 110 **Scott Erwert:** 92–93 **iStock:** 57 middle, 74–75 background
Jupiter: 13 **Picture Desk:** 23 (*I Was a Teenage Werewolf,* 1957 / AIP / The Kobal Collection); 27, 121 (*An American Werewolf in London,* 1981 / Polygram/Universal / The Kobal Collection); 36 (*Son of Frankenstein,* 1939 / Universal / The Kobal Collection); 44–45, 48 (*The Wolf Man,* 1941 / Universal / The Kobal Collection); 51 (*Teen Wolf,* 1978 / Wolfkill / The Kobal Collection); 53 (*The Company of Wolves,* 1984 / Palace/NFFC/ITC / The Kobal Collection); 55 (*The Wolfman,* 2009 / Universal Pictures / The Kobal Collection); 123 (*Abbott & Costello Meet Frankenstein,* 1947 / Universal / The Kobal Collection); 124 (*The Munsters,* 1964–1966 / CBS/MCA/Universal / The Kobal Collection); 129–129 (*Underworld: Evolution,* 2005 / Lakeshore Entertainment/Screen Gems / The Kobal Collection); 136 (*Cursed,* 2005 / Miramax / The Kobal Collection) **Wikipedia Commons:** 38, 68, 114

All image treatment and photo collaging by Scott Erwert

All illustrations by Scott Erwert with the following exceptions:
Juan Calle (Liberum Donum): 118

Front cover artwork by Scott Erwert